"Why, Miriam? Why is there so much bitterness within your heart?"

Miriam wiped away her tears, then said, "I suppose my bitterness began when William Graber moved away and fell in love with someone else. I loved him very much, and he made me believe that all men are alike. They cannot be trusted. When he broke my heart, I vowed never to allow myself to feel love for any man. I could not even trust God anymore. He could have prevented all of my pain and heartaches!" A sob caught in her throat, and Amos quickly wrapped his arms around her and held her against his strong chest.

When the sobs had finally subsided, Amos lifted her chin and looked directly into her eyes again. "I understand your pain, Miriam."

WANDA BRUNSTETTER is the wife of a pastor. They just recently moved from Idaho to Washington State. *A Merry Heart* is Wanda's first published novel.

A Merry Heart

Wanda Brunstetter

Heartsong Presents

Lovingly dedicated to the memory
of my sister-in-law,
Miriam (Mim) Brunstetter,
who always had a merry heart

A note from the author:
I love to hear from my readers! You may write to me at
the following address: **Wanda Brunstetter**
Author Relations
P.O. Box 719
Uhrichsville, OH 44683

ISBN 1-57748-250-6

A MERRY HEART

Cover illustration by Kathy Arbuckle.

PRINTED IN THE U.S.A.

one

Miriam Stoltzfus took one last look around the small one-room schoolhouse, then shut the door behind her. As she stepped outside, she could hear the voices of two children playing nearby, Sarah Jane Beechy and Andrew Sepler. The children couldn't see their teacher, she knew, for if they had, they surely would not have been having such a conversation.

"I wish our teacher wasn't so cross all the time," Sarah Jane said.

"My older brother says that she is just an old maid who never even smiles," Zachary added. "I think she must have a heart of stone!"

Miriam's cheeks burned hot, and she winced as though someone had slapped her face. Perhaps some of their words were true, she reluctantly admitted to herself. At age twenty-six, she was still an unmarried woman. This was nearly unheard of among the Old Order Amish group to which she belonged. Miriam shook her head. "I am not cross all of the time, and I do not have a heart of stone," she fumed to herself. But even as she spoke the words, she wondered if they were true or not. She was glad to see that the children had now left the school yard. She did not want them to know that she had overheard their conversation, nor did she feel in the mood to hear any more such talk against herself.

The horse and buggy, hitched under a tree nearby, offered solace to the tired schoolteacher. Speaking a few words of German-Dutch to the mare, she climbed wearily inside the box-shaped buggy. She would be glad to leave the school day behind and get home to her waiting chores.

A short time later, Miriam found her mother sitting on the front porch of their plain, white farmhouse, shelling fresh peas from their garden. "Look, Daughter, the first spring picking,"

Anna Stoltzfus called as Miriam stepped down from the buggy.

Miriam waved in response, then began the ritual of unhitching the horse. When she finished, she led the willing mare to the barn.

"How was your day?" Anna called, when Miriam reappeared a short time later.

Miriam crossed the yard and took a seat on the step next to her mother. "*Sis gute gange* (It went well)," she said in the German-Dutch language of her people. Then changing to English, she said with a long sigh, "It is so good to be home."

Anna wiped a wisp of graying hair away from her face where it had fallen loose from the tight bun she always wore under her head covering. "Problems at school?"

Miriam sighed again and squeezed her blue eyes tightly shut. After a few moments, she spoke. "It is probably not even worth mentioning, Mom, but after school I overheard two of my students talking. They seem to think that I have a heart of stone." She clasped her mother's hands in her own, nearly knocking the peas from the older woman's lap. "Oh, Mom, do you think it is true? Am I cross all the time? Do you think I really do have a heart of stone?"

Anna frowned. "Miriam, I do not think that any Christian's heart is made of stone. However, I have noticed that you are very unhappy, and your tone of voice is a bit harsh much of the time. Does it have anything to do with William Graber? Are you still pining over him?"

The color in Miriam's oval face turned a bright pink. "Of course not! I am certainly over him."

"I hope that you are, because it would do you no good to fret and dwell on what cannot be changed."

An uncomfortable yet familiar lump had formed in Miriam's throat, and she found that she couldn't bring herself to look directly into her mother's eyes. She was afraid the hidden pain in her own eyes would betray her words.

"If your troubled spirit is not because of your old beau, then what?" her mother asked.

Miriam shrugged. "I suppose everyone feels sad and out of sorts from time to time."

"Remember what the Bible tells us," her mother reminded. "'A merry heart doeth good like a medicine: but a broken spirit drieth the bones.' Happiness and laughter are good medicine for a troubled spirit, Miriam."

"I know, Mom. You have quoted that verse from Proverbs many times, but it's not always easy to have a merry heart." Miriam stood up, smoothing her long green cotton dress. "Now, if you will excuse me, I had best go to my room and change, and then I will help you with supper." She quickly went inside, leaving her mother behind on the porch with her head bowed in prayer.

&

Miriam's upstairs bedroom looked even more peaceful than usual. The freshly aired quilt on the bed was neat and crisp, giving the room the sweet smell of clean, outdoor air. The bare wooden floor was shiny and smooth as glass. Even the blue washing bowl that sat on the small dresser beneath the window reassured her of the cleanliness and orderliness of the plain room. On days like today she wished she could just hide away inside the four walls of her own room and shut out the world and all its ugliness.

Miriam took a seat on the comfortable bed and pulled her shoes off with a yawn and another long sigh. *How odd that some of the young people among my faith desire to leave this secure and peaceful life for the troublesome, hectic, modern way of life*, she thought. *I do not believe I could ever betray the Amish faith in such a way. Modern things may have their appeal, but simplicity and humility, though they separate us from the rest of the world, are a part of our culture that I treasure.*

She fluffed up her feather pillow and stretched out luxuriously for a few moments of rest before changing her clothes. Staring up absently at the plaster cracks in the ceiling overhead, she reflected again on the voices of the two children she had heard talking about her earlier. "How little they really do know about their teacher," she whispered. "They truly believe that I have a heart of stone. How can they know that my heart is really not hard like stone, but rather, it is a broken and shattered heart, and I am afraid it always will be."

A tear slid down Miriam's face and landed softly on the pillow beneath her head. She longed to be loved. To feel cherished. She knew in her heart that she was capable, or at least had been capable of, returning that same kind of love to a man who was willing to give his whole heart to her. She thought she had found that man in William Graber, but she knew now that no man could be trusted. She would guard her heart and never let another man cause her the kind of pain she was feeling now. The reminder of her past hurts was enough to keep her from ever falling in love again.

Miriam let her mind travel back in time. Back to when she was a pupil at the one-room schoolhouse, where she was now the teacher.

two

The young Miriam sat upright at her desk, listening attentively to the lesson being taught, until a slight tug on the back of her small, dark head covering caused her to turn around.

The deep green eyes of twelve-year-old William Graber met her own pale blue eyes and held them captive. Even then, at her young age, Miriam had known that it was love she felt for him. He was a good friend, but he was also the boy she hoped to marry some day.

William smiled and passed her the crumpled note he had taken from his shirt pocket. He had written it earlier that day, but he could not find the courage to give it to her until now, just a few short minutes before school would end for the day.

Miriam took the note and opened it slowly, not wanting the teacher to hear the paper rumpling. She smiled as she read the words. "Miriam: I want to walk you home from school. Please meet me by the apple tree out behind the schoolhouse. Your friend, William Graber."

Miriam nodded her agreement to William, then she folded the note and placed it securely inside her apron pocket. Impatiently, she waited for the minutes on the big battery-operated wall clock to tick away.

The walk home from school with William that day was the first of many. Over the next few years, they walked together, and he continued to carry her books, as well as continued to gain her favor. Their childhood friendship grew stronger with each passing year, until by the time they were both fifteen, their relationship had turned into a trusting love and a deep commitment to one another and to their future.

Their eighth year in school was their final one, and they both spent the next year in vocational training at home. William was instructed in the best of Amish farming methods, and Miriam learned the more arduous homemaking skills. After all, it was expected that they would marry some day and settle down on a farm of their own. They would both need to be taught well in all areas of farm life, as well as learn how to run an efficient and well-organized household.

William was given a horse and courting buggy at the age of sixteen. "Miriam, will you let me give you a ride home after the 'singing' at Schumans' tonight?" he asked after the morning church services that had been held in the home of his parents.

Miriam blushed from head to toe, though she really didn't understand why. They had been close friends for such a long time, but this was to be the beginning of their official courtship. "*Jah*, William," she whispered.

How her heart swelled with joy that night, as she prepared to go to the young people's "singing." She would be going with her two older brothers, Jonas and Andrew, but according to Amish custom, she would be allowed to accept a ride home from any eligible young Amish man. Since William had already asked her, the question of whom she might be traveling home with was already settled. She smiled to herself and placed her small covering securely on her head.

The "singing" was held in Schumans' barn, where the young people spent several hours singing some traditional Amish hymns, playing games, and enjoying a delicious array of foods, which had been prepared by the hostess and her daughters.

Miriam was having a good time, but she could hardly wait for the evening to end so that she could be alone with William. She was also anxious to experience the thrill of riding in his new, open courting buggy.

"I am riding home with William," Miriam whispered to her friend Crystal as they waited in line for refreshments.

"Ach, my, now that is not such a surprise," Crystal countered. "Everyone in this county knows that you two are sweet on each other."

Miriam blushed. "Hush. We are just supposed to be friends."

"Has he asked to come calling yet?" Crystal wanted to know.

Miriam shook her head. "Not yet, but then he only got his buggy a few weeks ago."

Crystal nodded and smiled knowingly. "Your brother Jonas only had his buggy two days before he asked to call on me."

Miriam giggled. "That sounds like my bold brother Jonas all right."

"I am so glad that my eighteenth birthday is only a few weeks away," Crystal said. "That way, if Jonas should ask me to marry him, I can be fairly certain that Papa will say, "*Jah,* it is fine with me and Mom." She smiled happily. "I know what my answer will be as well."

"I cannot speak for your papa, of course, but I do know my brother rather well. I think he is just counting the days until you turn eighteen."

Now it was Crystal's turn to blush. "I hope you are right. Don't you wish that you and William were a bit older, so you, too, could be thinking of marriage?"

Miriam giggled again and then whispered in her friend's ear, "I think we have both already thought about it, but we still have two more years to wait. I know that my parents would never let me marry before I turn eighteen."

&a

The ride home in William's buggy was everything that Miriam had expected it to be. A gentle August breeze offered the couple a cool but pleasant trip. The horse behaved well, responding to each of William's commands without delay. At one point, William was even brave enough to rein the horse with only one hand. That left the other hand free to seek out Miriam's.

Miriam felt the color come quickly to her cheeks. She smiled and stole a quick glance at her escort. She hoped that William couldn't see how crimson her face was in the moonlight.

William said nothing, but he smiled and tightened his hand around hers.

A short time later, as he walked her to the door, he whispered, "May I come visiting on Tuesday night, Miriam?"

Miriam nodded and ran quickly into the house. At last, they

were officially courting. She felt too joyous to even utter a word.

≈

The months melted into years, and by the time the young couple had turned twenty, there was still no definite wedding plans made. Though they often talked of it secretly, William did not feel quite ready for the responsibilities of running a farm of his own. After working full-time for his father since the age of fifteen, he wasn't even certain that he wanted to farm. He knew it was expected of him, but he felt that he might be more suited to another trade.

The opportunity he had been waiting for arrived when at the age of twenty-two, William was invited to learn the painting trade from his uncle Abe, who lived in Ohio. While Abe and one of his sons ran a small farm of their own, he also had a paint contracting business and needed another apprentice.

Miriam cried for days after William left, but he promised to write often and visit on holidays and some weekends. It wasn't much consolation to a young woman of marrying age. She had so hoped that by now the two of them would be married, perhaps even starting a family.

Impatiently, she waited for the mail each day, moping around in a melancholy mood when there was no letter, and lighthearted and happy whenever she heard from her beloved William. His letters were full of enthusiastic descriptions of his new job, as he explained in great detail how he had learned the correct way to use a paintbrush and apply paint quickly yet neatly to any surface. He told her about some of the modern buildings in town that they had contracted to paint. He also spoke of how he cared for her, and he promised he would be home soon for a visit.

William's visits were frequent at first, but after the first year was over, they became less and less, as did his letters. One day, on Miriam's twenty-fourth birthday, a long-awaited letter arrived with the familiar Ohio postmark. Her heart thumped wildly, and her hands trembled as she tore open the envelope. It was the first letter she'd had from him in several months, but the fact that it had arrived on her birthday caused her such joy that she nearly forgot how unhappy she had been feeling.

A sob caught in her throat, and she let out a gasp as she read the letter.

> *Dearest Miriam:*
>
> *There are no easy words to say what must be said in this note. You have always been a dear friend to me, and I will never forget the happy times we have shared. However, I will not be coming back to Pennsylvania, as I had originally planned. I have met a girl. Her name is Lydia, and we plan to be married in a few weeks. I am sorry if I have hurt you, but it is better this way. I could never have been happy working as a farmer. I know you will find someone else—someone who will make you as happy as Lydia has made me. I will always remember you and treasure the special friendship we had as children. I wish you the very best and God's richest blessings.*
>
> *Fondly,*
> *William Graber*

Miriam pulled her thoughts back to the present, and a familiar sob escaped her lips. That letter from William had come over two years ago, yet if felt like only yesterday. Her heart still ached when she thought of him. *How could he have found someone else?* she wondered even now. How could he possibly have thought that she would ever be happy again? How could he have referred to their relationship as a mere "childhood friendship"? He had left her with a broken heart, and she was certain that it would never be mended.

three

In the kitchen, Miriam found her mother rolling out a pie crust for chicken potpie. Anna smiled at her daughter and asked, "Are you feeling better now?"

Miriam reached for a clean apron hanging on a nearby wall peg and answered, "*Jah,* I am fine, Mom."

"Good, because we have guests coming for supper, and it would not be good if you were gloomy all evening."

"Guests? Who's coming over?"

Anna poured the vegetable filling into the pie pan before answering. "Amos Hilty and his daughter Mary Ellen."

Miriam rolled her eyes toward the ceiling. "Oh, Mom," she groaned. "You know I am not the least bit interested in Amos. Why must you go and scheme behind my back?"

"Scheme? Did I hear that someone in my house is scheming?" Henry Stoltzfus said as he entered the kitchen.

Miriam put her hand through the crook of her father's arm. "Mom is trying to match me up with Amos Hilty. She has invited him and Mary Ellen to supper again. They were just here last month, Papa."

Henry leaned his head back and laughed. His heavy beard, peppered generously with gray, twitched rhythmically with each new wave of laughter. "Daughter, it is high time that you married and settled down with a good man. Amos would make you a fine Christian husband, so do not close your mind to the idea."

"I think it is her heart that is closed," Anna said softly.

"If I *should* ever decide to marry, I would at least like to be the one to select my own husband!" Miriam exclaimed. She turned away and began setting the table.

Just then, Lewis, Miriam's younger brother, came in from outside. He hung his straw hat on a wall peg and sniffed the air appreciatively. "Something sure smells mighty good, Mom!"

"We are having company for supper, so please hurry and wash up," his mother instructed.

"Who's coming?" asked Lewis.

"Amos Hilty and his daughter," Miriam answered curtly.

"Ah-ha! I think Amos is a bit sweet on you, Sister."

"*Jah?* Well, I am certainly not sweet on him! Just because he's a widower, and his little girl needs a mother, does not mean that I am available, either! Why can't this family leave me alone? Can't you all see that I am perfectly content with my life just as it is?"

Lewis gave Mom a knowing look, and Mom smiled, but neither of them commented on Miriam's lengthy remark.

❧

Amos Hilty and six-year-old Mary Ellen arrived at the Stoltzfus house shortly after six o'clock. He entered the kitchen carrying his straw hat in his hands, while Mary Ellen carried a basket of freshly picked radishes. She smiled and handed them to Miriam. "These are from our garden," she announced happily.

"*Danki.* (Thanks.) I will slice a few for supper," Miriam responded. She took the basket and placed it on the cupboard, then turned back toward their guests.

Amos nodded at Miriam and gave her a broad smile. "It is good to see you, Miriam."

Miriam did not return the smile nor make any response, but rather went quickly to the cooler to get out some fresh goat's milk.

Amos shifted his long legs uncomfortably and cleared his throat. "Mary Ellen tells me that she is doing quite well in school. She says you are a good teacher."

"I do my best" was all that Miriam chose to say.

Miriam's parents and Lewis entered the kitchen from the parlor. "Good evening, Amos," Anna said warmly.

"Good evening to you as well. It was kind of you to have us to supper again."

"Mom knows how important good food can be for a man,"

Lewis said with a laugh.

"That is quite true," Amos agreed. He cast a glance in Miriam's direction, but she seemed not to notice.

"I think we should eat now," Henry said, pulling out his chair at the head of the table.

Everyone took their seats, and all heads bowed in a silent prayer of thanks for the food they were about to eat. Henry helped himself to the potpie and passed it to the guests, then followed it with a fine array of other homemade foods, including coleslaw, sourdough bread, sweet pickles, beet relish, and dilled green beans.

Mary Ellen's eyes scanned the table quickly. "You forgot my radishes, Teacher."

Miriam rose. "I'll see to it now." She excused herself and went to cut the radishes.

"Teacher is very pretty, don't you think so, Pappy?" Mary Ellen's blue eyes shone brightly, as she waited expectantly for her father's answer.

Amos nodded. "*Jah,* she is a fine-looking woman." He helped himself to another piece of potpie and smiled appreciatively. "The women of this house sure make a good supper."

Men! fumed Miriam inwardly. *They can't even express themselves without bringing food into the conversation. And children—they never know when to keep quiet.*

"Please, have some more coleslaw and bread," Anna offered.

"*Jah. Danki!*" Amos responded, as he reached for the bread basket.

Henry Stoltzfus laughed loudly. "You certainly do have a hearty appetite!"

Amos laughed, too. "I guess that comes from eating too much of my own cooking." He gave Miriam a quick glance, but she was staring down at her plate of half-eaten food.

Miriam was relieved when supper was finally over and the men had excused themselves to go to the front parlor for a game of checkers.

Mary Ellen sat on the floor playing with Boots, the cat,

while Miriam and her mother did the dishes. Miriam watched the small child out of the corner of one eye. Her brown hair, braided and pinned to the back of her head, looked a bit limp, as though it might come undone at any minute. Miriam tried to visualize Amos, his large hands clumsily trying to braid his daughter's long hair. She realized that it must be difficult for him to raise the child alone. There were so many things that only a woman could do well. He did need to find another wife—but certainly not her.

After challenging Henry and Lewis to several games of checkers and winning nearly every one, Amos finally decided that it was time to go home. As he started for the door with Mary Ellen by his side, he stopped and said to Miriam, "It was good to see you again. Maybe I will come by the schoolhouse soon."

"*Jah,* I am sure that Mary Ellen would like that," Miriam said. She felt fairly certain that Amos had intended his remark to inform her that he would like to see her again, but without being too rude, she wanted him to be aware that she was not interested in him in any way. She could only hope that he had gotten the message and would not show up at the schoolhouse.

four

One morning, several days later, Miriam received a surprise gift. Mary Ellen was the bearer, bringing to school a small pot of newly opened heartsease. "These are from Pappy," the child explained. "He said maybe some wild pansies would make you smile. You always look so sad, Teacher. God doesn't want us to be sad. Pappy said so." She placed the pot on Miriam's desk and hurried to her seat before Miriam had a chance to respond.

Miriam studied the delicate flowers. They were lovely, and the child was kind to bring them, but Miriam was irritated that Mary Ellen's pappy could look into her heart and see her sadness. *Perhaps I do seldom smile*, she thought, *but then, there must be a reason to smile. If God really wants me to be happy, then why did He allow William to hurt me so?*

Miriam looked away from the pot of flowers and tried to concentrate on the day's lesson plan that lay on her desk. She had more important things to do than ponder over the unexplainable.

❧

By the end of the day, a pounding migraine headache had overtaken Miriam. Fighting waves of nausea and dizziness, she leaned against the schoolhouse door with a sense of relief as she watched all the children file outside. She would be so glad to get home again, where she could lie down and rest.

Just as she was about to close the door, a buggy pulled into the parking lot. Amos Hilty stepped out, his large frame hovering above the small child who ran to his side. With long strides, he made his way to the schoolhouse, meeting Miriam just inside the door.

He removed his straw hat and smiled. "I came to pick up Mary Ellen, but I wanted to talk with you first."

Mary Ellen smiled up at her bearded father and reached for his large hand.

"Is there a problem?" Miriam asked.

Amos looked across the room at the flowers on Miriam's desk. "I see that you got the heartsease. Do you like them?"

"They are fine. Is there a problem?" Miriam repeated impatiently.

Amos shook his head. "Not unless you say no to my invitation."

"Invitation?"

"*Jah*. I was wondering—that is, Mary Ellen and I would like you to go on a picnic with us on Saturday afternoon. We were planning to go to the lake, and—

"*Mir sin so froh!* (We are so glad!)" Mary Ellen interrupted excitely. "It will be a lot of fun, and we will bring sandwiches and cookies. Maybe Pappy will even bring some homemade root beer. He makes it really good!"

Miriam tried to force a smile. Her throbbing head was spinning again, and she steadied herself against a nearby desk. "Thank you, but I really cannot go with you. Now, if you will please excuse me, I must be going home."

Amos stood there, his mouth open slightly, but no words would come. Still holding Mary Ellen's hand, he shook his head slowly and went out the door.

Miriam watched them go, noticing the look of rejection on Amos's face. Placing her hands over her aching forehead, she said aloud, "What is wrong with me? I know I was terribly rude to them. I did not even thank Amos for the flowers." Closing her eyes, she prayed, "Dear Lord, please take away this headache—and the pain in my heart."

When she arrived home a short time later, Miriam found her mother in the kitchen, peeling vegetables over the sink.

Seeing Miriam's face, Anna quickly pulled out a kitchen chair. "Sit down, Daughter. You do not look well at all."

Miriam placed the flowers on the table and flopped into the waiting chair. "I have another one of my sick headaches, Mom. They seem to be happening more often these days."

Anna went to the wood stove and removed the tea kettle,

already simmering with hot water. She poured some into a cup, and dropped a tea bag inside, then placed the cup in front of Miriam. "Drink a little peppermint tea to settle your stomach, and then go on upstairs and lie down for a while."

Miriam nodded. "That sounds nice, but what about the supper preparations?"

"I think I can manage without you this once. Anyhow, some day I will have to do it on a regular basis."

Miriam gave her mother a questioning look.

"When you are married," Anna explained.

Miriam sighed deeply and took a sip of the soothing herb tea. "I have no plans of marriage, Mom. Not now, and not ever!"

"My, what lovely pansies!" Anna said cheerfully, trying to change the subject. "Did one of your students bring them today?"

"*Jah.* Mary Ellen Hilty brought them. She said they were a gift from her pappy. It is just another one of his tricks to gain my approval."

"Miriam, please do not be so harsh. I am sure that Amos means no harm. He likes you, and he has no doubt been very lonely since his wife, Ruth, died over a year ago."

Miriam frowned. "He actually had the nerve to come by after school and invite me to go on a picnic with him and Mary Ellen this Saturday. I suppose he thought the flowers would pave the way."

"Did you accept his kind invitation?" Anna asked hesitantly yet hopefully.

"Of course not!" Miriam stood up abruptly. "I thought I had made myself quite clear, Mom. All he wants is a mother for his child, and someone to do all his cooking and cleaning. Well, I refuse to be that someone!"

Anna reached out and touched her daughter's hand lovingly. "I'm sure that Amos wants more than that, Miriam. He needs a friend and companion, just as you do."

"I do not!" Miriam shouted. "I do not need anyone!" Her voice broke, and she ran quickly from the room before Mom could see the unbidden tears on her face.

five

Early in the month of June, the farmer's market opened for business. It would remain open through the summer months and into the fall. The Stoltzfus family, though they no longer rented a booth for selling their wares, did enjoy going just to browse around and visit with many of their neighboring Amish friends and relatives. It was also an opportunity to get some good bargains on fresh produce, as well as a chance to purchase some new farming tools or look at the many hand-crafted items that were for sale.

The morning sun was already giving promise of a warm day, and as they drove into the parking lot, Miriam wiped the perspiration from her forehead and sighed deeply. She hoped that this summer would not be as hot and humid as last summer had been.

Henry Stoltzfus helped his wife down from the buggy. She smiled up at him and took his offered arm, then the two of them started off in the direction of the market building.

Miriam stepped down, followed by Lewis, who immediately began unhitching the horse.

"I am going on ahead," Miriam told her brother.

Lewis nodded. "*Jah,* sure, leave me with all the work! I can handle it, though. You run along and have all the fun." He laughed and gave his sister a playful swat on the arm.

Miriam shook her head. "Brothers!" She hurried toward the market, muttering to herself as she went.

She was halfway across the parking lot when she stumbled on a broken beer bottle that someone had carelessly tossed on the ground. Her legs went out from under her, and she fell hard, landing right on the broken bottle. "Ach, my!" she cried. She tried to get to her feet, hoping no one had seen her calamity. She also hoped that the nasty bottle had done no real harm to her long cotton dress or her knees.

Miriam felt two strong arms pulling her to an upright position. She looked up and found herself staring right into a pair of the brightest blue eyes she had ever seen.

"Are you all right, miss?" a young man with sandy blond hair asked, as he bent down to pick up the broken bottle.

The color in Miriam's face deepened. "I—uh—I am just fine, really—thank you."

"Your dress is torn, and I see blood showing through it. Let me see your knees. You might be cut up pretty bad," the man said.

Miriam wrinkled her forehead and tried to keep her voice from sounding too sharp or too loud. "I appreciate your concern, but I am just fine." She was not about to lift the hem of her cotton dress so that a man could see her knees. She was a woman of good upbringing, and he obviously was an Englishman of modern ways. What would he know of proper modesty? Besides, she didn't even know him.

Miriam looked down at her soiled skirt and rubbed her hand against it, as though in doing so it might take away the red stain and ugly tear. She took a few tentative steps and winced, but determinedly she went on.

"At least let me offer you some assistance." The young man put one arm around her waist without even waiting for her reply. "I'll walk you to the building. I assume that's where you were heading before your little accident?

"*Jah,* I was, but I can make it by myself." Miriam shook herself free from his grasp.

He smiled, showing his white teeth and an almost boyish grin. "My, my, I didn't know you Amish ladies could be so liberated. I thought you liked to have a man look after you."

"I am not liberated!" Miriam shouted. "But I do not need looking after, either!" Her eyes flashed, and ignoring the sharp pain in her right knee, she hurried on ahead.

The man walked on beside her. "I'm afraid we've gotten off to a rather bad start, miss. I'm sorry if I have offended you." He smiled and reached out a friendly hand. "I'm Nick

McCormick. Pretty catchy name, wouldn't you say?"

When Miriam made no reply, Nick went on, "I make it my duty to rescue fair ladies in distress."

Miriam found herself unable to keep from smiling. At least she thought it was a smile. The harsh frown was gone from her face, and she felt a bit more relaxed. She took the offered hand and shook it politely. "I am Miriam Stoltzfus, and I'm sorry if I was rude to you. Now, if you will excuse me, I really do need to catch up to my family."

"You're married then?" Nick asked boldly.

Miriam shook her head. "I was speaking of my parents." She wondered why she was even answering this man's personal questions. It was really none of his business who she was here with or what her marital status was.

"I see," Nick replied. "Then perhaps you wouldn't mind giving me a guided tour of the place."

Miriam gave him a questioning look.

"I'm a photographer for the *Daily Express*. I'm here to take some pictures for a cover story about the Amish," he explained.

Miriam noticed his camera bag hanging over one shoulder. She didn't know why she hadn't seen it there before. Her body stiffened, and the familiar frown was back on her face again. "I have no intention of acting as a tour guide so that you can photograph my people. It is against our religion to allow our pictures to be taken."

They had reached the market, and Nick dropped the bottle into a trash can and opened the door, letting Miriam step inside first. "I'm afraid it's my turn to apologize, Miriam. In spite of what you say, I'm aware that a few Amish people do allow pictures to be taken, especially of their children. I can see that you have your guard up for some reason, and I've obviously offended you by asking for your assistance. Please accept my apologies."

"It is of no real consequence. I get my feelings hurt a lot these days," Miriam said with a shrug of her shoulders. "Good day, Mr. McCormick." She turned and limped off in the direction of the ladies' rest room.

six

After inspecting her knees, Miriam found that only the right one was bleeding, but the cut did not appear to be too serious. She wet a paper towel and blotted the knee to stop the bleeding, then she tried unsuccessfully to get the blood off her dress. She was afraid to scrub too hard at it, for fear of tearing it more. It would have to wait until she got home to tend to it properly, she decided. She was thankful that the market had warm running water in the rest room. At home she would have had to stand at the sink in the kitchen and pump cold water for washing and then heat it on the stove if she wanted it to be warm. This was certainly much quicker and easier.

She was about to leave when the door flew open and a child burst into the room. It was Mary Ellen Hilty. "Teacher!" she cried excitedly. "I didn't know you were here today!"

"Actually, I just got here a short time ago," Miriam responded.

"Pappy will be glad to see you," the child said. "He likes you, Teacher. I can tell." Her hazel-colored eyes lit up, and her round cheeks took on a pink glow.

Before Miriam could think of a reply, Mary Ellen went on. "He thinks you cook good, too, Teacher. He said so."

Miriam tried to force a smile, but inwardly she was seething. *Of course he likes my cooking*, she thought. *He would like any woman's cooking. All he wants is a wife to take care of him and a mother for this poor little child. Well, if he thinks there is even a chance that I would marry him, he is terribly mistaken.*

"Are you happy to be out of school for the summer?" Miriam asked, hoping to change the subject to something other than Mary Ellen's pappy.

Mary Ellen smiled, a wide toothless grin. She had already

lost a baby tooth since school had been dismissed a week ago. "I like spending more time with Pappy, but I miss school— and I miss you, too, Teacher."

I would not be surprised if Amos told her to say that, Miriam fumed inwardly. "That was a very sweet thing to say, Mary Ellen," she forced herself to say.

"I meant it, Teacher. Some of the other children do not like you, but I think you are very smart—and pretty, too."

Another prompted compliment, Miriam thought. "Well, I must be going now, Mary Ellen. I need to look for my folks."

"Oh, they are talking to Pappy over by his root beer stand," Mary Ellen was quick to say. "Why don't you go and try some? I am sure Pappy would give you a glass for free."

"Thank you, maybe I will." Miriam left the room and turned quickly in the opposite direction, away from the side of the market where all the refreshments were sold.

She didn't have to go far before she saw a familiar face. Her best friend and sister-in-law, Crystal, was coming toward her. Holding each of her hands were her two-year-old twin boys, Jacob and John.

"Aunt Mimmy, *schussel* (hurry)!" Jacob squealed.

"Aunt Mimmy, *schussel*!" John repeated.

"How are you little rascals?" Miriam asked in German-Dutch, the only language that Amish children under school age could speak. She knelt down next to her nephews, but the pain in her knee caused her to wince. Carefully, she stood up again.

"Miriam, what is wrong? Are you hurt?" asked Crystal.

"It is not really serious. I just had a little fall outside in the parking lot. I cut up my knee a little, and I embarrassed myself some, too." She made no mention of the brazen young man who had offered her assistance. Why bring more questions from Crystal?

Crystal looked down at Miriam's dress. "You have torn your skirt. Let's go find your mom. Maybe she has something we can mend it with. Your folks are here with you, aren't they?"

"*Jah*. I am told that they are over at Amos Hilty's root beer stand."

"Let's go find them then," Crystal suggested. "Maybe after Mom fixes your dress, she will agree to watch the twins for a while, and then we can go off by ourselves and do some shopping together. It will be just like old times."

The idea of some time alone with Crystal did sound nice, but Miriam wasn't eager to see Amos. She hesitated before answering. "Why don't you go on? I will meet you over by the quilts. I would really like to look at some that Karen Freisen has for sale."

"That sounds good, but what about your dress?" Crystal asked.

"It can wait until I go home," Miriam answered.

"Well, come with us anyway, and I will treat you to a nice cold root beer," Crystal said.

"*Schnell* (quickly), Aunt Mimmy!" John said loudly.

"*Schnell!*" echoed Jacob.

Miriam shrugged. "Oh, all right, I can see that I am outnumbered. Let's go get us some root beer."

Amos, his tall frame hovering above those around him, was pouring a glass of frothy root beer when Miriam arrived with Crystal and the twins. He handed the glass to the young boy who was his customer. When he looked up, his deep brown eyes met Miriam's. He smiled a warm friendly smile. "Hello, Miriam. It's good to see you again. Your folks were here a few minutes ago. You just missed them."

"Oh, wouldn't you know it! I wanted Anna to watch these two little guys for me," Crystal told him.

"Maybe we should go try to find them," Miriam was quick to suggest.

Jacob began pulling on his mother's skirt, and John pointed toward the root beer.

"*Jah,* boys, we will have some root beer first," promised their mother.

Amos opened the spigot on the root beer keg, and then he served up four glasses of icy cold soda. Two were in large glasses for the ladies, and the twins got smaller glasses, just right for boys their size.

Frothy foam got all over John's and Jacob's noses when they took a drink, and the grown-ups all laughed—even Miriam. It felt good to laugh. It was something she seldom did anymore.

After the drinks were finished and they had engaged in some polite conversation, Miriam suggested that they be on their way. Amos nodded, saying that he hoped to see her again soon.

"He is definitely interested in you," Crystal whispered as they walked away.

"*Jah*? Well, I am definitely not interested in him!" was Miriam's firm reply. "Furthermore, it troubles me the way everyone is always trying to match us up. Even his daughter, Mary Ellen, is in on the little plot."

Crystal put her hand on her sister-in-law's arm. "Mary Ellen is a very sweet child. I am sure that no such plotting ideas have ever entered her young little mind."

"Maybe not, but some adults, whom I will not bother to mention, are in on the plot to marry me off to Amos Hilty, and some of them are using that poor child as an instrument of their devious ways."

Crystal laughed. "How you do exaggerate, my dear friend. No one is being devious or plotting against you. We all just want your happiness. Surely you can see that."

Miriam didn't answer, so Crystal went on. "Ever since we were children, all we could think about or talk about was how we would marry some day and have a family. We both knew how happy we would be if God gave us good husbands and some fine children to raise."

"That is easy for you to say," Miriam snapped. "You are happily married to my brother, Jonas, and you have these adorable twins to fill your life. I, on the other hand, am an old maid schoolteacher, and I plan to stay that way!"

seven

The morning sun, beating against the windows, was already warming the Stoltzfus kitchen when Miriam came downstairs. She squinted against the harsh light that was streaming through an open window. Her head felt fuzzy; another pounding migraine had sent her to bed early the night before, and the unpleasant remnants of it still remained. What she really needed was something to clear her head of the dusty cobwebs that lingered there from her disturbing sleep. Perhaps she would wash her hair and then go down by the lake to dry it. Some time alone in the early morning sun would surely do some good. Papa and Lewis were already out in the fields, and Mom had gone over to her eldest son Andrew's place to help his wife, Sarah, with some baking. No one would need her for anything. This was the perfect chance to be alone so that she could think and pray.

She cut herself a thick piece of shoofly pie, while she waited for the kettle to heat. She ate the molasses-filled breakfast pie hungrily, then washed it down with a big glass of fresh goat's milk, taken from the cooler. The quietness of the house seemed to soothe her aching head a bit. She liked solitude. In fact, she really preferred being alone.

By the time she had finished eating, the water was warm enough. She poured it into a ceramic basin, which she placed inside the sink. After pouring some of it onto her long brown hair, she lathered up her scalp with a bar of Mom's homemade lilac soap. A hint of the perfumed flower drifted up to meet her nose, and Miriam sniffed appreciatively. She rinsed with the remaining warm water, then reached for the big towel she had placed nearby on the cupboard. She blotted her hair dry, being careful not to rub too aggressively, which she knew would only aggravate her headache.

When Miriam was satisfied that the majority of water had been absorbed from her hair into the towel, she wrapped a clean towel loosely around her head, picked up her hairbrush from the wall shelf nearby, and went out the back door.

The lake was clear and blue, and the sun had warmed the grassy shoreline. Miriam took a seat on the carpet of green and slipped off her shoes. She wiggled her toes in the grass and sighed. *Sometimes I wish I were still a child.*

She reached up and pulled the towel from her head, causing her damp hair to fall loosely about her shoulders. She shook her head several times, letting the glowing sun warm her tresses. She closed her eyes and lifted her face toward the sky.

Dear Lord, she prayed, *if only my life could be simple and pleasant, as it was when I was a small child. Why must my heart hurt so? I want to be pleasing in your sight, yet I know that most of the time I fall terribly short. How can I have a merry heart, as Mom says I should, when I am so full of pain?*

A tear squeezed through a closed eyelid, and Miriam reached up to wipe it away.

The cracking of a twig nearby caused her to jump. She turned and saw the lens of a camera peeking through the branches of a willow tree. When she realized that it was pointed directly at her, she gasped and jumped quickly to her feet.

Nick McCormick stepped out from behind the tree. "Sorry if I startled you, miss."

"How dare you!" Miriam shouted. "I thought I had seen the last of you at the market yesterday."

Nick smiled sheepishly. "Uh-oh, it's the liberated Amish woman I had the privilege of helping to her feet yesterday morning. And what beautiful feet they are, too, I might add." He smiled and bowed to her. "I certainly had no idea that I'd be seeing that fair maiden again today. Especially not like this."

Miriam pulled the hairbrush from her apron pocket and began quickly brushing her tangled hair. "I must look a sight," she said, but even as she spoke the words, she wondered why she should care what she looked like. Nick McCormick was just an arrogant and very bold Englishman.

"I really do not appreciate you sneaking up on me," she continued. "And I certainly do not like the fact that you were taking my picture. I told you yesterday—"

"Yes, yes, I know. The Amish don't believe in being photographed. I heard that it's something about graven images or some such other foolishness." He smiled again and moved closer to her.

Miriam felt the need to move away from him, but she held her ground instead. Why should she give him the impression that she was nervous in his company? "It is not foolishness! The Bible tells us in Exodus twenty, verse four, 'Thou shalt not make unto thee any graven image.' We believe that includes taking photographs or displaying them."

"I can see that you certainly are well versed in the Scriptures," Nick said, as he took a seat on the grass and began to advance his camera to get ready for the next picture. "Well, I say the Bible is just a lot of fairy-tale hogwash! And furthermore, I'll have you know that I've photographed several Amish children, and they didn't put up such a fuss. Is their religion any different than yours?"

Miriam sat down, making sure that she was now a comfortable distance from the insolent intruder. Her hair was almost dry, and it lay in gentle waves across her shoulders and down her back.

"Children do not always know any better," she told Nick. "Besides, you English folks usually bribe them with money or candy. They are not strong enough to say no."

Nick laughed, causing his blue eyes to twinkle. "How about you, Miss Stoltzfus? Would you allow me to photograph you for a piece of candy?"

"Don't be ridiculous! I would not allow my picture to be taken for any price!" Miriam paused and looked the man squarely in the eyes. "Anyway, you have already taken my photograph without my knowledge or my consent. I am sure that you probably have some prize-winning shots of the silly Amish woman drying her hair by the lake."

Nick's face sobered. "I've offended you again, haven't I?"

"*Jah.* To be perfectly honest, you have" was her curt reply.

Without saying a word, Nick opened the back of his camera and removed the exposed film, then he handed it to Miriam. "Here. Accept this with my heartfelt apology for intruding on your privacy."

Miriam closed her fingers around the roll of film and smiled slightly. "Thank you for understanding, Mr. McCormick."

"I'm not sure that I really do understand. I know one thing, though—you're really beautiful when you smile," Nick told her. "And please, call me Nick," he added.

Miriam felt the color rising to her cheeks. No one had ever told her that she was beautiful before. William used to say that she had a kind face, but never beautiful. She looked down at her trembling hands.

"Now I've embarrassed you," he said. "I must apologize once more."

Miriam looked up. "It is just that— Well, no one has ever called me beautiful before."

Nick smiled a warm, sincere smile. "Then that was their mistake." He rose to his feet. "I'd better get going. I have to be back at the newspaper office before noon." He held out his hand. "It's been nice talking to you again. I hope this won't be the last time we meet."

Miriam shook his hand. "Good-bye, Mr. McCormick—I mean, Nick." She watched silently as he walked away and wondered why her heart was beating so rapidly against her chest.

eight

August was a hot month, and everyone found it difficult not to complain about the stuffy, humid air. There were days when not even so much as a tender breeze graced the valley.

One evening a summer storm finally brought wind and rain, but it only caused the air to be more humid than it had been before. Miriam found it even more difficult not to be cross and complaining. She sat on the front porch steps, watching the streaks of lightning brighten the sky.

"God's handiwork is a pretty picture, is it not?" said a deep voice from behind her.

She turned to see her father standing on the porch, stroking his long, full beard. He smiled at Miriam. "God is quite the artist, wouldn't you say?"

She nodded and smiled slightly. Her father had such a way with words, and such a love and understanding of God. He saw God's hand in everything around him, things that others would have simply taken for granted.

"We needed a good rain," Henry Stoltzfus said as he took a seat on the step beside Miriam.

"I suppose so, but it is making the air awfully muggy," she replied.

"*Jah,* well we can put up with a little mugginess when the good Lord answers our prayers and brings the rain. The summer crops were in much need of a good soaking."

Miriam couldn't argue with that. She knew how important the crops of alfalfa, corn, and tobacco were to all the Amish farmers in the valley. She reached for her father's hand. "You always see the good in things, Papa."

Her father squeezed her hand. "'As a man thinks in his heart, so is he,' the Bible tells us."

Miriam couldn't argue with that, either. Perhaps that was

why she was so unhappy. She thought unhappy thoughts. But how did one go about making themselves think pleasant thoughts?

Miriam shuddered as a clap of thunder sounded a bit too close to the house.

"Is something besides the storm troubling you, Daughter?" her father asked.

Of course something is troubling me. Something is always troubling me, she thought. Miriam shook her head. "Just the storm. I hope the lightning doesn't hit anyone's house or barn."

"*Jah,* that is always uninvited," her father agreed. "But if it should happen, we will certainly rebuild." He laughed lightly. "A good barn raising is always a joy."

"A joy?" Miriam's voice was tinged with sarcasm. "You mean, it is a lot of work!"

"*Jah,* that, too, but working together with your friends and family is a joyous time."

Miriam didn't say anything more. What was the use in arguing with such a positive man as her father? She had to admit she admired him for his optimistic attitude. Why couldn't a little of it rub off on her?

❧

On Sunday, church services were held at Andrew and Sarah's home. Their farm was only about three miles from the senior Stoltzfus's place, so the ride by horse and buggy was a rather short one.

After Papa helped Mom down from the buggy, he and Lewis went to join his other sons, Jonas and Andrew, behind the barn, where the horses were all hitched in the shade. Miriam and her mother made their way to the front porch to visit with Sarah, Crystal, and some of the other women who had already arrived. The twins were playing with their cousins, Rebekah and Simon, on the front lawn, along with several other small children.

It was another warm day, and Miriam was thirsty. "I am going to step inside the kitchen for a drink of water," she whispered to her sister-in-law Sarah.

Sarah, who was rocking baby Sally, answered, "Help yourself. There is a pitcher of lemonade in the cooler, if you would rather have that."

Miriam shook her head. "*Danki,* but water will suit me just fine."

When she entered the kitchen, she thought that it was empty, but then she saw someone across the room, standing near the sink. It was Amos Hilty. He was bent over Mary Ellen, scrubbing her face with a wet washcloth. The child was wiggling and squirming, and she heard Amos say, "Mary Ellen, please stop *rutshing* (squirming)!"

When the child spotted Miriam, she squealed and ran to her side. "Teacher! You look very pretty today. Doesn't she, Pappy?"

Miriam looked down at her own dark purple cotton dress, with a black apron worn over the front of it. She wondered what there was about her that the child thought was pretty; in spite of herself, she remembered Nick McCormick's comment about her being beautiful. Her eyes met Amos's, and he smiled.

"Your teacher is a fine-looking woman," Amos said to Mary Ellen.

Miriam made no response.

Amos shifted his long legs nervously. "Mary Ellen sampled some of Sarah's raspberries from the garden when we first arrived," he said. "She had sticky red juice all over her face."

Miriam nodded. "I came in for a drink of water. I will get it and be out of your way."

Amos stepped away from the sink. "Help yourself to the pump. I have done about as well as I can with this little scamp's dirty face anyway."

Miriam went to the cupboard and got out a glass, then she went to the sink, where she pumped out just enough water to quench her thirst. She wished that Amos would go outside and leave her alone, instead of standing there watching her.

"Will you sit at the table with Pappy and me during lunch after church?" Mary Ellen asked.

Miriam had to think quickly. "I believe my family is expecting me to eat with them."

"Mary Ellen, why don't you run outside and play now," Amos said suddenly. "I want to speak with your teacher."

The child gave him a questioning look, but obediently she went out the back door, looking back over her shoulder to flash a winning smile at Miriam.

The last thing Miriam wanted was to be alone with Amos Hilty. She looked around the room, hoping that someone else would enter and rescue her from the determined man who stood by her side.

Amos pulled out a kitchen chair and motioned for Miriam to sit down. Reluctantly, she obliged, and Amos took a seat directly across from her.

"Church will be starting soon," Miriam reminded.

Amos glanced at the wall clock. "We still have some time yet. I want to discuss something with you."

"About Mary Ellen?"

"No, about us."

"Us?" Miriam's voice sounded harsh and high-pitched, even to her own ears.

"*Jah*. It is about our relationship."

Miriam looked directly into Amos's serious brown eyes. She cleared her throat to stall for time. She wanted to be sure that her words were well chosen. "The only relationship we have is the fact that your daughter is one of my students. So, if this little talk is not about Mary Ellen, then what?"

Amos stood up and began pacing back and forth across the kitchen floor. "Miriam, surely you have been able to tell that I have an interest in you," he said.

Miriam's mouth dropped open. She hadn't expected such a bold declaration from him.

Amos hurried on. "I want to spend more time with you—to come courting. Yet every time I ask you to go someplace with Mary Ellen and me, you have an excuse why you can't. Whenever I try to talk to you, you are unfriendly and act as though you are trying to avoid me."

"I am sure that you mean well, Amos," Miriam replied, "but isn't the real truth that you really just want a mother for your little girl?"

Amos looked stunned. "Miriam, I—"

"You need not deny it, Amos Hilty," Miriam interrupted. "Everyone knows that you are a widower, without any family around to help you raise your daughter. It is understandable that you would want to find a wife to help care for her."

Amos looked down at the toes of his boots. "I—that is—I know that Mary Ellen is quite taken with you, Miriam. In fact, you are all that she talks about when she returns from school each day. However, I do have some concerns about the type of influence you could have on her young mind."

"What are you saying?" Miriam asked.

"I am saying that you are quite melancholy, and I had hoped that if we started courting you might find more joy in life, and—"

"Now wait just a minute!" Miriam shouted. "Do you actually believe that you are such a wonderful person that just courting you would make me happy and delightful enough to have around your daughter?"

"That is not what I meant to say, Miriam." Amos sat back down at the table again. "I find you quite attractive, and I think that we could get along rather well together if you would just give it a chance."

Miriam stood up abruptly and started across the room. She turned back and said, "There are several available Amish women in the valley, Amos. Some are a bit younger than me, perhaps, but I am sure that if you use your charms on one of them, you might persuade her to be your wife."

"But, I—" Amos stammered.

Miriam turned away from him and went out the door, slamming it on the way out.

nine

"Heartless. . .Heartless. . .Heartless. . ." The sound of the buggy wheels echoed in Miriam's ears as though they were calling out to her and reminding her of the heartless way she had behaved toward Amos that morning.

She probably had hurt his feelings by telling him that she was not interested in him and that she knew he was only after her because of Mary Ellen, but at the time she hadn't cared about his feelings. She had such pain in her own heart because of William Graber, and now Amos was hurting her by using his own child to try and gain her favor. How foolish did he believe her to be? She had been fooled by a man once, only to have her heart torn asunder. No, she would never allow herself to be hurt like that again.

When the Stoltzfus family arrived home from church, Miriam helped her mother bring their lunch dishes inside, then she hurried up to her room, saying that she wanted to change her dress. The truth was, she needed to be alone for a while. She was beginning to feel another one of her headaches coming on, and rest was the only thing that ever seemed to help.

The following day after lunch, Miriam and her mother were busy cleaning up the kitchen. The men had gone back out to the fields to work, leaving the women alone with a sink full of dirty dishes.

Anna Stoltzfus watched her daughter as she filled the sink with hot water from the stove. "The men were certainly hungry, weren't they?" she said, trying to make some idle conversation.

"*Jah.* Just look at all the watermelon rinds in the bowl on the cupboard. I think Lewis ate three or four pieces himself."

"Our men do have some pretty hearty appetites," Mom

agreed. "Speaking of men—I was talking with Amos Hilty yesterday, right after the worship service. He asked me—that is, he was wondering if I would speak to you on his behalf."

Miriam dropped the wet dishrag into the soapy water so hard that it sent several large bubbles drifting toward the ceiling. "I do not believe this!" she cried. "Doesn't that man ever give up? I thought I had made myself quite clear to him yesterday. Obviously my words must have fallen on deaf ears!"

"Now, Miriam, please calm down," her mother said soothingly. "I have probably made a mistake bringing this up, but Amos was very upset after he talked with you yesterday."

"*Jah,* I can just imagine."

"He is afraid that you may have the wrong impression of him—of his intentions, that is," Anna continued.

"Oh, his intentions are very clear. At least to me, they are!" Miriam said loudly. "Mom, can't you see it, too? He just wants a housekeeper and a mother for Mary Ellen."

"I'm sure he wants more than that."

"Oh, *jah*! He wants someone to darn his socks and cook his meals, too. Well, that someone is not going to be me!" Miriam shouted.

Anna reached out and placed a loving hand on Miriam's trembling arm. "Miriam, is it so wrong for a man to want those things? They are all part of the married life, you know."

"Then let him get a hired girl or someone else to help out. Just tell Amos for me that I want to be left alone!"

"I believe that he does have a hired girl come in part-time, and you know that Amos has no relatives to call on. His parents are both deceased, and his two brothers both have farms of their own to run. I am told that his in-laws live in another state, so—"

"I am truly sorry about all of that," Miriam interrupted, "but it is really not my problem. And it is certainly not reason enough for me to marry Amos Hilty!"

"Has he asked you to marry him?" Mom asked hopefully.

"Well, no, he just asked to come calling, but—"

"I think he only wants to establish a friendship with you for now, Miriam. In time you will both know if there is a chance for love or marriage."

"I can already tell you that there is no chance for either love or marriage. Not for me, at least," Miriam stated flatly. She marched across the room and picked up the big ceramic bowl. "I'm going out to the pasture to give these rinds to the cows."

❧

Out in the pasture, the herd of dairy cows grazed contentedly. They perked up their ears when they saw Miriam coming. She dumped the watermelon rinds over the fence, then stood watching as several of them ate greedily.

"Ach, my, you silly old cows. You carry on as though you haven't a thing to eat," she scolded. "See here, you have a whole pasture of green grass to eat!"

She lingered for a while, watching the mothers with their young ones. She was in no hurry to get back inside to more of Mom's meddling. She was glad that September was only a few weeks away, and school would be starting up soon. She was looking forward to teaching again. Being at home all summer long gave her too much time to think. Even though there were always plenty of chores to do, it wasn't the same as keeping her brain busy. Besides, when she was around home more, Mom seemed to meddle in her life more.

Miriam leaned on the fence rail and watched with interest as a mother cow began washing her baby with her big rough tongue. For some reason it reminded her of the sight she had witnessed when she'd stepped into Sarah's kitchen and found Amos scrubbing his daughter's face. The baby cow was squirming about, just as Mary Ellen had done.

"I suppose all little ones need a mother to take care of them," she whispered. "Mary Ellen is such a sweet child. For her sake, I hope that Amos does find a suitable wife—but it certainly won't be me!"

ten

The first day of school was always a little hectic and unorganized. There were several new children in class, and since they were first graders and knew only their Pennsylvania German-Dutch language, they needed to be taught English. This took extra time on the teacher's part, and it meant that the older students must do more work on their own.

Mary Ellen Hilty was in the second grade and already knew her English fairly well, but still she lacked the discipline and attention span to work on her own for very long. From her seat in the second row, she raised her hand and called, "Teacher! Teacher, I need your help."

Miriam gave her an impatient look. She was busy teaching Joanna Jost and Nona Shenk the letters of the alphabet, and she did not want to be disturbed.

"Teacher!" Mary Ellen called again.

Miriam put her finger to her lips to quiet the child. "One minute, Mary Ellen. I will be with you in just a minute."

Mary Ellen nodded and smiled. She folded her hands and placed them on top of her desk, as she waited patiently.

When Miriam was finished with her explanation to Nona and Joanna, she went over to Mary Ellen and squatted down beside her desk. "What is it, Mary Ellen?"

"I do not know what this word is." The child pointed to the open primer in front of her.

"That word is grandfather," her teacher answered. "You must learn to sound it out. Gr-and-fa-ther."

Mary Ellen looked up at Miriam. Her hazel eyes were very large. "My grandpa and grandma Zeeman live far away. grandpa and grandma Hilty live in heaven with Jesus. So does Mama."

Miriam noticed a sadness about the child's face that she

40

had never seen before. Usually there was a light in her eyes and a warm smile on her lips. For a moment she allowed herself to feel pity for the young girl. She had no one but her father to look after her. No one but him to love.

The smile was quickly back on Mary Ellen's face. "Thank you for helping me, Teacher."

Miriam touched the child's arm lightly. "You are welcome."

Back at her own desk, Miriam found herself watching Mary Ellen instead of grading the morning spelling papers that were lying before her. The child never actually looked unkempt, but her hair always showed telltale signs of not being secured tightly enough in the braided knot at the back of her head. Her face was always scrubbed squeaky clean, which came as no surprise to Miriam after watching Amos wash the child's face on that Sunday morning in Sarah's kitchen.

Miriam shook her head, bringing her thoughts back to the present. She had no desire to think about that day or to be reminded in any way of the things that Amos had said to her. Regardless of everyone's denial, she knew that Amos's interest in her was purely selfish. A mother for his child was what he wanted the most. Though Mary Ellen was a dear child, and Miriam had to admit that she did have a soft spot for her, it was certainly not enough reason to marry, or even to court the girl's father. If she did ever marry, it would have to be for love, and that possibility seemed seriously doubtful.

Mary Ellen looked up then and smiled at her teacher. It was a warm, heart-melting smile, and Miriam found herself fighting the urge to go to the child and hold her in her arms. For one brief moment, she wanted to tell her that she would marry her father and be her new mama. That she would love her and take care of her needs. Instead, she just smiled back at Mary Ellen, then quickly turned her attention back to her spelling papers. What on earth had she been thinking of? she wondered. The idea was absolutely absurd!

The children always looked forward to lunchtime. When the teacher pulled the rope for the noon bell, she would be caught up in a stampede of children as they made a mad dash for their brightly colored lunch buckets. Today was certainly no exception, and Miriam fumed as she was nearly knocked over by one of the older boys.

"Slow down once!" Miriam exclaimed. "You don't need to be in such a *shussel*!"

Kenneth Freisen grunted an apology and hurried to his seat with his lunch bucket.

It only took about five minutes for the children to gobble down their lunches and scamper outside to play for the remaining twenty-five minutes of lunch break. Games of baseball, drop-the-hanky, and hopscotch could be seen being played around the school playground.

Miriam stood at the window, watching the children and wondering if the ache she felt between her temples would turn into another one of her pounding migraine headaches. The day was only half over, and already she felt physically and emotionally drained. She wondered if teaching was really her intended calling in life. She often ran out of patience with the children, and when she felt as she did today, she wondered if perhaps her mother was right. Maybe she should find a husband and settle down to being just a homemaker and wife.

"What am I doing?" she chided herself. "Even if I did want to get married, which I do not, I am not in love with anyone, and I will never marry without love or trust—both of which I do not feel for Amos." She shrugged and decided that her mood was only because it was the first day of school; in a few days, when everything became a routine again, she would be glad that she was teaching school.

Miriam's thoughts were interrupted when a ruckus broke out in the school yard outside. Several children were laughing and shouting, and many were standing around in a large circle.

Miriam hurried outside to see what the noise was all about. Several of the children pulled away from the crowd when they saw their teacher approaching.

"What is the trouble here?" Miriam asked Kenneth Freisen, who stood nearby.

"Aw, it is just some of the girls. *Sie Sin glene Bapel Meiler.* (They are little blabbermouths.)"

Miriam pulled two of the girls aside, and that was when she saw Mary Ellen Hilty standing in the middle of the circle. Tears were streaming down her round cheeks, and she was sniffing between sobs.

"Mary Ellen, what is it? Are you hurt?" Miriam asked with concern.

"It's all right. They did not mean it, I'm sure," Mary Ellen said quietly. She managed a weak smile through her tears.

"Who did not mean it? Did someone hurt you?"

"She is just a little crybaby," Kenneth Freisen stated. "She can't even take a bit of teasing."

Miriam eyed him suspiciously. "And who was doing this teasing, might I ask?"

"It wasn't me, Teacher. It was the girls. Like I said before, they are blabbermouths."

"Very well, which of you girls was involved, and what were you teasing Mary Ellen about?" Miriam asked impatiently. The pain in her head was increasing, and she feared the dizziness and nausea that usually followed would soon be upon her as well.

The cluster of children became suddenly very quiet. Not one child stepped forward to announce his or her part in the teasing.

Miriam frowned and rubbed her forehead. "Very well then, the entire class shall stay after school for thirty minutes."

"But, that's not fair, Teacher! Why should we all be punished for something that just a few girls said?" Kenneth said loudly.

"*Jah,* I didn't do anything, and I'll be sent to the woodshed if I'm late," Karen Lederach whined. "My papa doesn't like tardiness."

"My mama has chores waiting for me," Grace Seitz said.

Miriam looked at Mary Ellen. "What about it, Mary Ellen? Won't you tell me now who is guilty and what they said?"

Mary Ellen shuffled her feet nervously, then let her tear-stained eyes rest on her teacher's face. "I will tell you in private what they said, but I cannot say who said it. It would be tattle-taling, and Pappy doesn't like a tattletale. He has said so many times." She smiled. "Besides, the Bible tells us to do to others as we would have them do to us. I wouldn't want someone to get me in trouble."

Miriam led her inside the school building and looked down into the little girl's sad face. "All right, Mary Ellen. Please tell me now what this was all about."

Mary Ellen looked up at her. "The children notice that I don't dress like them. My pappy. . .he doesn't always know how things should go and neither do I. Today I had my dress on backwards and I never even knew it." She bit her lip. "That's why some of the children were laughing. But please don't punish them."

Miriam nodded reluctantly. "You have set a good example for the entire class, Mary Ellen." She helped Mary Ellen to put her dress on the right ways around, and then she went back outside and looked at each of the other children. "I hope you have all learned something today. No one will be required to stay after school this time, but if this ever happens again, I will punish the entire class. I don't care if you all have to go to the woodshed when you go home. Is that quite clear?"

All heads nodded in unison.

"Now get on back to your play. Lunchtime will be over soon." Miriam smiled at Mary Ellen, and the child smiled back.

She really is a dear girl. Mary Ellen, the heartsome, Miriam mused. *Even in the face of adversity, she still has a loving heart. I wonder how she does it?*

eleven

The days of September went by quickly, and Miriam fell back into her role as teacher, just as she had done for the past several years. She still had days of frustration and tension, leading to her now familiar sick headaches, but at least she was busy, and she was doing something that she felt was worthwhile and meaningful.

One afternoon, after school had been dismissed for the day, Miriam decided to pay a visit to Crystal. It had been awhile since they had taken the time for a good visit, and she was certainly in need of one now.

When Miriam pulled her horse and buggy to a stop in front of Jonas and Crystal's farmhouse, she saw Crystal outside removing her dry laundry from the clothesline. Miriam called to her, and Crystal turned and waved, then motioned for Miriam to follow her inside the house.

Crystal deposited the laundry basket on a kitchen chair and pulled out another one for her sister-in-law to sit on. "It's so good to see you. You have been on my mind a lot lately and also in my prayers."

"Oh, really? Why is that?"

Crystal shrugged and began to fold the clothes in the laundry basket. "I have been praying for your happiness" was her simple reply.

"Perhaps it is not meant for some to be happy," Miriam said with a deep sadness in her voice.

"I do not believe that for a moment, and neither should you," Crystal answered firmly. "We have been taught since we were children that life offers each of us choices. God gave us all the ability to choose what we will think and feel. He expects the believer to make the right choices and choose to follow Him. He expects us to be happy and content with our lives."

45

Miriam frowned. "That is easy for you to say. You are happily married to a man you love deeply, and you have two beautiful little boys. How could you not be happy?"

Crystal dropped back into the basket the towel she was holding and pulled out a chair next to Miriam. After taking a seat, she reached out and took one of Miriam's hands. "Please do not be envious of my life. You can have the same happiness as well."

Miriam stood up suddenly, nearly knocking over her chair. "How dare you speak to me like that! I thought that you were supposed to be my best friend!"

"I—I am," Crystal stammered.

"Then do not talk to me as though I am a child."

"I wasn't. I mean, I don't think of you as a child," Crystal said. "I was merely trying to tell you—"

"That I should marry someone?" Miriam interrupted. "Were you thinking of Amos Hilty, perhaps? Listen, I have some news for you, friend. Marrying that man would never make me happy! He does not love me. All he wants is a mother for Mary Ellen and, of course, someone to do all of his cooking and cleaning. Furthermore, I certainly do not feel any love for Amos!"

"Sometimes one can learn to love," Crystal said gently.

"Did you have to *learn* to love my brother?"

"Well, no, but—"

Miriam interrupted again. "I came here because I needed to be with my best friend. Can't we please change the subject and just enjoy each other's company?" She went to the sink and got herself a glass of water. She was beginning to feel another headache coming on.

"Of course we can change the subject," Crystal was quick to agree. "I am very sorry if I upset or offended you. It's just that I want you to be as happy as I am."

"Please, do not worry and fret over me. I am doing just fine without a husband, and who cares if I'm not truly happy anyway? I have come to accept the fact that life is not always meant to be a bowl full of sweet cherries. I—" She broke off as she heard a horse and buggy pull into the yard, and she went to look out the window.

"Who is it?" Crystal asked.

Miriam peered out the window. "It looks like Lewis. Maybe he's looking for me. Mom probably sent him to tell me that she needs my help. It is getting pretty close to supper time."

Crystal glanced at the clock across the room. "You're right. I am surprised that the twins aren't up from their naps yet."

There was the sound of a man's boots on the back porch, then suddenly the back door flew open, and Lewis burst into the room.

Miriam could not remember ever seeing her younger brother look so upset before. He almost looked as though he was afraid of something. Even as a child, he had always been the brave and fearless one.

"What is it, Lewis?" Miriam cried. "You look as though you've seen something terrible."

Crystal pulled out a chair for him. "Here, you had better sit down."

"No, there is no time," Lewis said breathlessly. "We have got to go *schnell*!"

"Go where?" Miriam asked.

"To the hospital," Lewis replied. His voice quivered, and it was obvious that he was close to tears.

"The hospital? Is someone ill? Who is it, Lewis? Tell us, please." Miriam's tone was pleading.

"It's Papa. He—he was working in the fields with me, and everything was just fine—at least I thought it was, but suddenly Papa turned very pale, clutched at his chest, then he just fell over."

Miriam gasped, and Crystal waited silently as Lewis continued. "It took everything we had, but Mom and I finally got him into the buggy, and then we went straight to the hospital."

"What is it? What do the doctors say is wrong with Papa?" Miriam asked.

Lewis shook his head. "They are still running tests, but they think it might be his heart."

"A heart attack?" Crystal asked.

Lewis nodded. "Where is Jonas? He should be told, too."

"He is still out in the fields with my pa. If you and Miriam want to go on ahead to the hospital, I will send Jonas as soon as he comes back to the house."

"I'll leave my buggy here and ride with Lewis, if that's all right," Miriam said to Crystal.

"*Jah,* of course. We will see that it is brought back to your place later," Crystal answered.

Lewis reached for Miriam's arm. "I have already notified Andrew, and he is on his way to the hospital. Let's go now, before it's too late."

"Too late? What do you mean, too late? Is Papa's condition that serious?" Miriam's face was pale, and her eyes had grown large and pleading.

Lewis nearly pushed her toward the door. "The doctors are not sure, but Papa isn't even conscious, and—"

"You two hurry along then," Crystal interrupted. "Jonas will be there soon. I expect him any minute."

"Seind Papa eingedenkt in Gebeth! (Remember Papa in your prayers!)" Miriam called over her shoulder.

twelve

Henry Stoltzfus's condition proved to be very serious. The doctors confirmed that he had suffered a massive heart attack. His wife and four children stood around his bed as the doctor gave the shocking news that because his heart was so weak, he would probably not survive the night, though they would do all they could for him.

"But, how can this be?" Anna Stoltzfus cried. "My Henry has always been a very strong, healthy man!"

"Sometimes as we get older—" the doctor began.

"Older? My papa is only fifty-seven years old!" Miriam shouted. "He is not old, and he is not going to die!" She shook her finger in front of the young doctor's face.

"Miriam, please calm down," Jonas said soothingly. He put his arm around her waist and pulled her off to one side. "If it is the will of God, Papa will live. If not—"

"If not, then what? Do we all just put on a happy face and go on living as though Papa had never been a part of us?" Miriam shrieked.

"Miriam, please do not do this," Mom said tearfully. "We all need to remain calm. We need to pray for Papa."

Miriam's thoughts suddenly drew inward. How many times had she prayed over the last several years? How many of her prayers had God answered? Had He kept William from falling in love with someone else? Had He given William back to her? Surely He could have caused William to change his mind and return to Pennsylvania. Had God made the pain in her broken heart go away?

Miriam felt so weary of praying and receiving no answers. Still, she knew in her heart that prayer was the only chance her papa had now. So, she would pray, and she would even plead and bargain with God. Perhaps He would trade her life for Papa's. If she was gone, she would not be so greatly missed, but Papa was badly needed by all the family, and especially by Mom.

"I will be out in the waiting room, praying," she whispered to Mom. "Send Lewis to get me if I am needed or if Papa wakes up." She glanced at her father's still form, lying on the cold hospital bed, hooked up to machines and an IV needle. Quickly, she ran from the room.

The waiting room was empty when Miriam entered. She was glad for the chance to be alone. Silently, she began to pace back and forth, going from the window to the doorway and back again, pleading with God to heal her father.

At one point, Miriam stopped in front of the window and stared out at the street below. Several cars were parked along the curb, and several more were driving past. Some children rode bicycles on the sidewalk below. A bird flew past the window and landed in a nearby tree. The world was still going about its business as usual. It was a world that she and her Amish family had chosen to be separate from, based on the biblical teachings of nonconformity. Yet now, due to unwelcome circumstances, here they were being forced to accept the modern ways in order to provide her father with the best medical care available. Home remedies and herbal cures would simply not be appropriate for something so grave as a heart attack. But would modern medicine be enough? Could these doctors, in their fancy up-to-date hospital with all its machines and gadgets, really save Papa's life and bring him back to them again? If, by some miracle of God, he did get well enough to come home, would he ever be whole and complete, able to work on the farm again?

The waiting room door swung open suddenly, interrupting Miriam's thoughts and prayers. Jonas and Andrew both stood in the doorway, their faces pale and somber. "Papa is gone," Andrew said in a near whisper.

Papa is gone. Papa is gone. The dreaded words echoed inside of Miriam's head. Once more her prayers had gone unanswered. Once more her heart would ache with pain. It wasn't fair. Life wasn't fair! Without even a word to either of her older brothers, she ran from the room.

Tears blinded Miriam's eyes as she stumbled down the long hospital corridor. Her only thought was to run away—to escape from this awful place of death, though she had no idea where she was going. She passed by the elevator, not wanting to bother with the modern convenience, and ran quickly down two flights of stairs. She opened the door, which led outside, and was just about to step out into the evening air, when she ran directly into a strong pair of arms.

"Hey there, fair lady! You just about knocked me off my tired feet!"

Miriam looked up into the deepest pair of blue eyes that she had ever seen. They were mesmerizing eyes—the kind that make a woman's heart beat hard and fast inside her chest. She knew those eyes. "Mr. McCormick!"

Nick McCormick smiled broadly, showing off a set of straight, white teeth. "We do seem to keep bumping into each other, don't we, Miriam Stoltzfus?"

Miriam could only nod, as she reached up to wipe away her tears.

"And please," Nick continued, not seeming to notice her tear-streaked face, "dispense with the formalities of Mr. and just start calling me Nick."

Miriam moved away from the tall, blond-haired man who stood in front of her, blocking the exit door of the hospital. She had no desire to make conversation with the Englishman, and she certainly did not want him to see how upset she was.

"If you will excuse me, I was on my way out," Miriam managed to say.

"I can certainly see that. You almost ran me over." Nick looked at her seriously. "Sorry, I didn't notice before, but I can see now that you are upset. Is there something I can do to help? I really do enjoy rescuing damsels in distress, you know." He winked.

"I—uh—am fine. I mean, I will be all right if I can just get some fresh air."

"Then air you shall have, fair lady." Nick stood to one side and politely opened the door so that Miriam could walk through.

Once outside, she took several deep breaths, allowing the cool evening air to fill her lungs and clear her head. Her legs took her quickly down the sidewalk and away from the hospital.

thirteen

"Slow down. What's your hurry?" Nick called, as he hurried to keep up with Miriam.

Miriam turned to see him directly behind her. "I thought I was alone. I mean, I didn't know you had followed me," she stammered.

"Do you mind?" Nick asked.

"Don't you have business at the hospital?" she asked, avoiding his question.

Nick shrugged. "I was there to cover a story about an old man who was beaten and robbed at a convenience store."

"Oh, how awful! Maybe you should—"

"It can wait," Nick said quickly. "Right now, I think maybe you need someone to talk to."

"Front page headlines or a back page article?" Miriam asked sarcastically.

"You insult my integrity, fair lady. I have no intention of conducting a newspaper interview with you. I just thought you could use a strong shoulder to cry on and maybe even a little heartfelt sympathy."

Miriam sniffed indignantly. "What makes you think I need any sympathy?"

Nick reached down to wipe away a tear that still lingered on her cheek. "You've been crying."

Miriam knew that she could not deny her tears. She also knew that she really did need someone to talk to. "*Jah,* I have been crying," she admitted shakily. "My papa just died of a massive heart attack."

"Then shouldn't you be with your family at a time like this?" Nick asked.

Miriam nodded. "*Jah,* but I have no words of comfort to offer any of them. I just want to be alone."

"Oh, I see. You want to be alone in your misery, is that it?" Nick asked bluntly.

"*Jah,* exactly," Miriam surprised herself by answering. She began to walk briskly again, hoping to leave the obstinate man behind. Perhaps she did not need his listening ear after all.

But the newspaper reporter was not to be put off so easily. He kept in step with her and even offered her his arm, though she declined with a shake of her head. "Let's go somewhere for a cup of coffee," he suggested.

"I told you—"

"Yes, I know—you'd rather be alone," Nick finished her sentence. "Maybe that is how you think you feel, but I think if you search your heart, you'll discover that what you really need is someone to talk to. I promise not to include our conversation in my next article on the Amish—and I won't take any pictures." Nick laughed, and even Miriam had to smile slightly though her throat was thick with tears.

"Oh, all right," she conceded. "I suppose a cup of coffee could do no harm."

The little cafe that Nick picked was just a few blocks from the hospital, and it was nearly empty when they stepped inside. They took a seat at a booth in the far corner, and Nick ordered them both a cup of coffee and a piece of apple pie.

Miriam declined the pie, saying that she wasn't hungry, but Nick insisted that she needed the nourishment and that it would make her feel better if she ate something.

Miriam found the man's controlling ways to be very irritating, yet for some strange reason, she allowed him to have his way. She gave in and ate the pie, finding that she was actually hungry after all.

"Feeling better?" Nick asked, as he watched her eat the piece of pie.

Miriam nodded. "At least my empty stomach does. I had no supper tonight. After school let out, I stopped to see my sister-in-law for a few minutes. I planned to be home in plenty of time to help Mom with supper, but then my brother, Lewis, came by and told us that Papa had collapsed while he was at work in the fields. We all rushed to the hospital, and— Well, you know the rest."

Miriam took a deep breath and shook her head slowly. She could not believe that Papa was really gone, and she couldn't believe that she was sitting here in a cafe, with a man she barely knew, pouring out her heart to him. Maybe that was why she felt free to do it, because she didn't really know him. He had no expectations of her. He would make no demands on her emotionally.

Nick reached out and took her hand, and she made no effort to stop him or to take her hand away. The comfort that he offered felt good. It was something she hadn't felt in a very long while.

"I think I understand how you must feel," Nick said softly. "I lost my own dad when I was just nine years old. I was an only child, and Mom and I had it pretty rough for several years."

"How did you manage?" Miriam asked.

"It was hard. We lived with my grandparents for a few years. They looked after me while Mom went back to school for some training. She became a nurse, and then she was able to support us by working at a hospital in Chicago. That's where I'm from." Nick scratched his head thoughtfully with his free hand. "Those were some tough times, all right, but I think they helped to strengthen me."

"Where is your mother now?" Miriam asked.

"She's still living in Chicago. When I was about fifteen, she remarried. I never got along very well with her new husband, so after I finished high school, I went to a college out of state. I majored in journalism, and after college, I worked at several small newspapers. When the newspaper here in Lancaster offered me a job, I took it." Nick smiled at her and winked. "And you know the rest of the story."

Miriam could feel her cheeks turning pink. It had been so long since she'd been in the company of a young, good-looking man. She had forgotten how pleasant it could feel, and now, with her heart aching, his attention was like balm.

Nick McCormick had actually made her forget about her grief for a few brief moments. "Do you live here in Lancaster alone, or are you—?"

"Married?" Nick finished her question.

She nodded, wondering what on earth had caused her to be so bold, or for that matter why she even cared whether he was married or not. She quickly pulled her hand out of his and nervously reached up to straighten her head covering.

Nick laughed. "No, I'm not married. It's not that I have anything against the state of matrimony. Guess I've just never met a woman who captured my heart enough to make me want to settle down and start a family." He winked again. "Of course, any woman who could put up with me would have to be a real gem."

Miriam smiled nervously. "I think maybe I should be getting back to the hospital now. My family might begin to think that I have deserted them."

Nick nodded, his eyes sympathetic.

"That you for your kindness, Mr. McCormick—I mean, Nick. I do feel better after talking to you. But the days ahead will be difficult ones." She gulped. "I don't know how we will manage without Papa—but you have reminded me that pain and death touch everyone's lives at some time or another. I feel fortunate that I am not an only child. I know that my three brothers will help out, and at least Mom won't have to support herself. And, of course, I will be there to help with some of the extra chores."

"Do you have a job outside the home?" Nick asked.

"*Jah,* I am a schoolteacher."

"That's right, you said earlier that you were on the way home from school when you found out about your father," Nick said. "I don't imagine that an Amish teacher makes much though."

The magic of the moment was suddenly gone, and Miriam's mind came back into proper focus. "I make enough!" she snapped. Her blue eyes flashed angrily.

"No, hold your horses, fair lady. I meant no harm in asking

about your wages," Nick said, holding one hand in the air, as though he was asking for a truce. "I was only trying to show my concern for your situation. If you hadn't been so quick to cut me off, I was about to say that if there is ever anything I can do to help you or your family, please feel free to call me at the newspaper office."

"That is very kind of you," Miriam said, her voice softening some, "but we Amish always help each other in times of need, and—"

"And you're not used to asking favors of modern Englishmen?" asked Nick.

"Mr. McCormick—I mean, Nick, I really do appreciate your kind offer, and I thank you for your listening ear tonight. I'll think about calling you if I should ever need your help."

Nick smiled and stood up. "I'd better pay for our eats, then I'll walk you back to the hospital."

"Really, there's no need," Miriam was quick to say. "I can find my own way back."

Nick shook his head. "You Amish are sure a proud people, aren't you? Have you forgotten that I have an interview at the hospital? I was going in as you were going out," he reminded her.

The walk back to the hospital was a silent one. When they entered the building, Miriam extended her hand to Nick. "I thank you again for your kindness to me."

Nick returned the handshake. "It was all my pleasure, Miriam. I'm only sorry for the circumstances." He squeezed her hand gently, then turned toward the information desk, then back to her again. "Don't forget my offer of help. Should you ever need the listening ear or the services of a worldly Englishman, just go to your nearest phone booth and call my office."

fourteen

The days following Henry Stoltzfus's death were dark ones. First, there was the funeral and all the preparations that went with it. Miriam had never lost anyone close to her before. When her Grandmother Gehman died, she had only been five years old. She hardly even remembered her mother's mother at all. And Grandpa Gehman, who moved to Illinois shortly after his wife's death, had passed on nearly ten years ago, when Miriam was still a young teenage girl. She had never been close to her maternal grandfather and really did not know him very well. Neither of their deaths had affected her the way that Papa's had. Both of his parents were still alive, though living in another county with Papa's oldest brother. It was not natural for aged parents to outlive their children.

Just three short days after Papa's death, Miriam stood with her friends and family and watched as his plain pine box was taken from the horse-drawn hearse and set in place at the burial site. She closed her eyes tightly, trying to block out the memory of her final look at Papa's face. Dressed in traditional white, his body had been available for viewing during the two-hour funeral service, which was held at the Stoltzfus home before the burial. Though the local undertaker had done a fine job, Miriam's father no longer looked like himself. The stark reality that he was truly gone was more than she could bear.

Why, Lord? Why? she asked God now, as a tear slipped beneath her closed eyelids. *How could you have taken Papa from us?* She opened her eyes and glanced to her right, where she saw her mother, openly weeping as the bishop said the final words over her husband of thirty-five years. Was Mom really strong enough to make it without Papa? Miriam wondered. Would she herself be able to offer Mom the kind of emotional support that she would need in the days to come?

With a heavy heart and a firm resolve, Miriam decided right then that she must have a determined heart. Through her own sheer will, she must put her grief and pain behind her so that she could be strong for Mom and the rest of the family.

When the burial service was finally over, everyone in attendance climbed back into their waiting buggies, and forming a single line, they all followed the Stoltzfus family back to their farm, where they would spend the remainder of the day eating and offering words of comfort and encouragement to the bereaved.

Miriam didn't feel very hungry, but rather than draw attention to the fact that she wasn't eating, she put a sandwich, some dilled cucumbers, and a piece of gingerbread cake on her plate. After picking up a glass of iced tea, she quietly made her way to the lake, where she could be alone. Friends and family had been dropping by the house for the last three days, and today all the Amish families in the valley seemed to be present. She needed some quiet time, away from all of the sympathetic looks and words that were meant to be helpful.

The lake was always beautiful in the early fall. While the days were still warm, nighttime often brought with it a light frost, gently kissing the trees with crimson color.

Something about the peacefulness of the lake made her think of Nick McCormick, perhaps the fact that she and Nick had visited with each other in this same spot several months before.

Miriam blushed, just thinking about how the obstinate man had sneaked up on her with his camera, and how he had taken her picture with her hair down and uncovered. *Now wouldn't that have made a fine photo for the* Daily Express? she thought to herself.

What was there about Nick that made her feel these unexplained emotions, anyway? She had only seen him on three occasions, and each time he had succeeded in making her angry, but he'd also made her smile. She had even opened up and talked to him in spite of her great pain in losing Papa.

Nick was not one of her people, yet she felt closer to him than she had to any man in such a very long time.

William Graber had been the only man Miriam had ever shared her thoughts or feelings with, and when he left her for another woman, she vowed never to let herself get close to another man. While she wasn't exactly close to Nick McCormick, she had let him a little closer to her than she had any other man since William. Was it simply because he was so easy to talk to, or was it because he was an outsider, and she knew that there was no threat of a possible commitment?

Miriam's thoughts were interrupted when a male voice suddenly called out her name. She looked over her shoulder and saw Amos Hilty heading toward the lake. He was alone and was carrying a plate of food.

"I thought you might like something to eat," Amos said, when he reached the lake shore.

Miriam held up her half-eaten plate of food. "I am afraid I have not eaten what I already have. I guess you will just have to eat it yourself."

Amos laughed and took a seat on the grass beside her. "I already had one helping, but I suppose I could force myself to eat another. All this home-cooked food sure does whet the appetite. I am not really much of a cook, so I don't enjoy my own meals very much."

If that was a hint, it is wasted on me, Miriam thought to herself. "Where is Mary Ellen?" she asked.

"She is busy playing little mother to your twin nephews," Amos answered. "Since she is occupied, I decided to sneak away and check up on you."

"What makes you think I need checking up on?" Miriam asked, a bit too harshly.

Amos cleared his throat. "Well, it's just that— I know what it is like to lose someone close to you, and I thought that I might have some words of comfort to offer." He reached out a large, well-callused hand and touched Miriam's shoulder lightly. "I am so sorry about Henry. He will be missed by all of the Amish community, as I am sure he will be sorely missed by his family. He was a good man."

Miriam knew in her heart that Amos was only trying to console her, but for reasons unknown even to her, she felt irritation instead of comfort from his words, and even his very presence made her edgy. Somewhere in the back of her mind, she wondered if he had an ulterior motive for his kindness. If he could win her heart with sympathy, then he might be able to gain her approval and perhaps even convince her that she needed a husband. Of course, Miriam reasoned, in reality, it was he who needed a wife. Someone to cook and clean for him. Someone to be a mother to his young daughter.

Miriam stood up quickly, brushing away the pieces of grass that clung to her cotton dress. "I really should be getting back to the house. Mom may be needing me."

Amos's deep brown eyes revealed his hurt, but Miriam tried not to notice. Maybe if she gave him the cold shoulder often enough, he would finally understand that she was not now, nor would she ever be, interested in him.

"Thank you for your kindness, Amos," Miriam added briskly, "but I am going to be fine, really. Life is full of hardships and pain, but each of us has the power within us to rise determinedly above our troubles and take control."

"The power within is God," Amos reminded her.

Miriam made no reply. Instead, she turned to go, then momentarily turned back and said, "I will help my family through this great time of loss."

"But what about you, Miriam? Who will help you in the days ahead?"

"I shall help myself!" Miriam turned around again, and this time she ran as quickly as she could. She needed to be as far from Amos Hilty as possible.

"Wann dumich mohl brauchst, dan komm Ich," Amos whispered. "When you need me, I will come."

fifteen

The routines of life must go on, even for those in mourning. With Papa gone, Lewis had to work twice as hard to keep up with all of the farm chores. The alfalfa fields needed one final harvesting before winter set in, and the job was just too big for one man. Even with the use of modern machinery, it would have been a challenge, but horse-drawn plows made the work harder and more time-consuming. Andrew and Jonas pitched in to help, coming over early in the morning before doing their own chores, then returning again in the evening. Some of the neighboring Amish men also came to help. Miriam wondered how long they could keep it up and still maintain their own homes and jobs. Surely their families were suffering from their absences.

Mom, too, kept busier than ever as she worked tirelessly from sunrise to sunset. While it was true there was more work to do now that Papa was gone, Miriam suspected that the main reason her mother kept so busy was so that she would not spend all her waking hours thinking about Papa and how much she missed him. Often in the middle of the night, Miriam would be wakened by the sound of her mother crying. Her parents had had a good marriage, and Mom would probably never get over Papa's untimely death. If only there was some simple way to erase all the pain in one's life, Miriam often found herself thinking.

❧

The fall harvest was finally completed, and everyone's workload had lightened just a bit. Lewis assured his older brothers and neighbors that he could manage the farm chores on his own now. Without too much argument, they all agreed that it would not be necessary for them to come over every day. They returned to their families and their own routines, reminding Lewis that he should call on them anytime he felt the need.

One afternoon, in early November, Miriam dismissed her students early because of the threat of a storm. Angry-looking dark clouds hung over the schoolhouse yard, and the wind whipped madly against the trees. A torrential rain was sure to follow. By letting the children go now, they might all make it home before the earth was drenched from above.

"I'll give you a ride home," Miriam told her six-year-old niece Rebekah. "Wait for me out by my buggy."

Rebekah smiled. "*Ich will mit dir Hehm geh.* (I want to go home with you.)" Impulsively, she gave her aunt a hug and ran out the schoolhouse door.

Miriam hurriedly erased the blackboard and was about to write the next day's assignment on it, when a loud clap of thunder sounded. The small one-room schoolhouse shook, and then a terrible snapping sound rent the air, followed by a shrill scream.

Miriam rushed to the door. A sob caught in her throat when she saw that Rebekah was lying on the ground next to her buggy, a large tree limb lying across her back. "Oh, dear God," she prayed, "please let her be all right."

Rebekah was unconscious when Miriam got to her. There was a gash on her head, with some bleeding, but Miriam could not tell the full extent of her injuries. She felt so helpless and alone. All the other children had already left for home. There was no one to help her and no one to tell her what to do. She knew that the child must be taken to the hospital to be examined, but she was afraid to move her, lest she cause more damage. She knew there was a pay telephone booth just a mile or so down the road, but if she went to call for help, Rebekah would have to be left all alone.

Miriam seldom found herself wishing for modern conveniences, but right now she would have given nearly anything if there had been a telephone inside of the schoolhouse. "Oh, Lord, what should I do?" she prayed, as she wrapped a piece of cloth from her apron around Rebekah's head. The young woman with a determined heart, who only a few short months ago had decided she could handle all of life's problems on her own, suddenly realized that she needed God's help. "Lord, I do not ask this for myself, but for the dear, sweet child who lies at my feet. Please send someone now, or I must leave her alone and go for help."

Suddenly, Miriam heard the sound of an approaching buggy. She held her breath and waited as it came into sight, then she rushed toward it when it entered the school yard.

The driver of the buggy was Amos Hilty, who explained that he had come to pick up Mary Ellen because of the approaching storm.

"Oh, Amos, Mary Ellen has already gone on home. I let all the children go early because of the bad weather. But a tree limb fell on my little niece Rebekah, and now she is lying on the ground unconscious. I was so frightened to leave her alone and go for help." Miriam's voice shook with emotion, and her breath came out in short, raspy gasps.

"Let's put her in my buggy, and we will take her to the hospital," Amos suggested.

"Oh, no! I don't think she should be moved. What if something is broken? What if—"

"Very well then, you wait right here with the child, and I will go call for help. There is a pay phone just down the road."

Miriam nodded. "Please hurry, Amos. She hasn't opened her eyes at all. I think it might be very serious."

❧

It seemed like hours until the ambulance arrived, but it had only been about twenty minutes from the time that Amos had gone. The wind was still howling, but fortunately the rain held off until right after Rebekah, who had been strapped to a hard, straight board with her neck wrapped in a large collar, was placed safely inside the back of the ambulance.

"I need to go to the hospital with her," Miriam told Amos, who had returned to the schoolhouse to offer further assistance. "But someone needs to notify Andrew and Sarah."

"You ride along in the ambulance, and I will go by my farm and get Mary Ellen, then I will go tell your brother and his wife what happened."

"My buggy. What about my horse and buggy?"

"I shall see that they get safely home for you." Amos reached out and touched Miriam's arm lightly. "Try not to worry. Just pray, Miriam. We must trust God in situations like this."

Miriam nodded and climbed numbly into the back of the waiting ambulance.

As the ambulance pulled out of the school yard with its siren blaring, Miriam looked back and saw Amos climbing into his buggy. "I never even told him thank you," she whispered.

ta

After several hours of testing, the doctor's reports were finally given to Rebekah's family. The news was very grave. The child had a concussion and a bad gash on her head where the tree limb had hit. That was no doubt the reason for her still being unconscious. But even worse news was the fact that Rebekah's spinal cord had been severely injured, and if she lived, she would never walk again.

Miriam choked back a sob when the doctor gave them the shocking news, and Sarah began to cry hysterically. Andrew put his arms around his wife and tried to comfort her, but he, too, had tears running down his cheeks. It was much too hard for any of them to accept. First Papa's heart attack, and now this. How much did the Lord think that one family could take? Why would He allow such a thing to happen to an innocent young child? Miriam asked herself.

"I—I am so sorry," Miriam told her brother and his wife. "If only I had not asked her to wait for me—" Her voice broke, and she ran from the room in tears.

As Miriam made her way quickly down the hospital hallway, she felt like she was reliving the past—the terrible night that she had fled the hospital when Papa died. When she opened the door that led to the street, she half expected to see

Nick McCormick standing there. But he wasn't there this time to offer her words of comfort and a listening ear. Suddenly, she remembered his last words to her. "If there's anything I can do to help you or your family, please call me at the newspaper," he'd said.

Should she call? she wondered. Would Nick really be able to help her? Should she even be turning to an outsider for comfort and support? Surely it wasn't wrong to reach out for help when one was in need. Miriam turned the corner and headed for the pay phone at the end of the block. Her head was pounding, and her fingers shook as she dialed the number of the *Daily Express*.

"Hello. May I speak to Nick McCormick? He is a reporter at your newspaper," Miriam said into the receiver.

"One moment, please," the woman's voice on the other end of the phone said.

Miriam held her breath and waited anxiously until finally she heard "This is Nick McCormick. How may I help you?"

"It is Miriam Stoltzfus, Mr. McCormick—I mean, Nick. You said that I should call if I ever needed anything."

"That I did, fair lady! What can I do for you?" Nick responded warmly.

Miriam reached up to rub the side of her pounding temple. She hoped that she wasn't about to be sick. "I—uh, that is—I need to talk. Can we meet somewhere?"

"Where are you now?" Nick asked.

"Just a block or so away from the hospital."

"The hospital? Are you all right?"

"It is not me. It is—" Miriam's voice broke.

"Miriam, whatever has happened, I am so sorry," Nick said softly. "Remember the little cafe where we had coffee a few months ago?"

"I remember," Miriam managed to say.

"Meet me there in fifteen minutes," Nick told her. "You can tell me all about it then."

sixteen

The cafe was full of people when Miriam arrived. A quick look at the clock on the far wall told her it was the dinner hour. Her eyes sought out an empty booth, but there was none. She stood there nervously as all eyes seemed to be upon her. Was it the fact that she was wearing plain clothes that set her apart from the rest of the world? she wondered.

"May I help you, miss?" a man's voice called from behind the counter.

"I—uh—that is, I am meeting someone, and we need a table for two," Miriam stammered.

"The tables and booths are all filled, as you can probably see, but you can take a seat on one of the stools right here at the counter, if you would like."

Not knowing what else to do, Miriam took a seat, as he had suggested. She began to look at the menu the man handed her, but nothing really appealed. How could she have an appetite for food when her niece was lying in the hospital, unconscious, with the prospect of being a cripple for the rest of her life? Rebekah could even die, they had been told.

Miriam looked up when a firm hand was placed on her shoulder. "Nick! How did you get here so quickly?"

Nick shook his head. "It's been over thirty minutes since we talked, and I told you fifteen. I'm actually late, fair lady, and I'm sorry to have kept you waiting."

Miriam glanced at the clock. "I guess I lost track of time."

Nick looked around. "It's really crowded in here. Was this the only seat you could find?"

Miriam nodded. "I'm afraid so. I have been waiting for one of the booths, but no one seems to be in much of a hurry to leave."

"Are you very hungry?" Nick asked.

"No, not really, but I could use something to drink, and maybe some aspirin." Miriam rubbed her forehead.

"Headache?"

She nodded. "I get really bad migraines whenever I'm under too much stress, and I don't have any White Willow Bark herb capsules with me. They usually help."

"I'll get you some iced tea to go," Nick offered. "I've got some aspirin in the glove box of my car. How about if we go for a ride? We can talk better if we have some privacy, and I don't think we'll get any in here."

"I—I suppose it would be all right," Miriam said hesitantly.

"I know that you Amish aren't supposed to drive a car, but it's okay for you to ride in one, isn't it?" Nick asked.

"*Jah,* but only when it is absolutely necessary," she replied.

"You did say that you needed to talk. That's necessary enough for me," Nick told her.

"All right then," Miriam agreed. "But I should not be gone too long. I left my brother and his wife at the hospital, and I didn't even tell them where I was going or when I would return."

"I promise not to keep you out past midnight, Cinderella." Nick winked at her gravely, then he ordered an iced tea to go.

Miriam blushed and tried to hide it by hurrying toward the door.

Nick's car was a new red and black, sporty-looking sedan. Miriam could smell the aroma of new leather as she slid into the soft passenger seat. "You have a beautiful car," she said in a near whisper.

"Thanks. Too bad it's not paid for yet," Nick answered. He reached inside the glove box and pulled out a small bottle of aspirin. "Here, take a couple of these."

Miriam took the bottle and opened it. As she swallowed the pills with the iced tea he had purchased for her, Nick turned on the ignition and pulled away from the curb. "So, do you want to tell me what's bothering you, or would you rather just ride around for a while?" he asked.

Miriam clutched the side of her seat with one hand while

hanging onto her tea with the other. "Going at this speed, I am not sure that I can think well enough to speak."

Nick smiled. "Come, come now. I'm only doing thirty-five! Now, if we were out on the tollway, I could see you getting a bit nervous. I even get stressed out sometimes during rush hour traffic."

"I know it's silly, but remember, I am used to riding in a horse-pulled buggy," Miriam replied.

"How about if I pull over at the park, and you can just sit and relax while you tell me what has happened?" Nick offered.

"That—that would be fine, I suppose." Miriam pulled nervously on the corner of her dark green cotton dress. She wasn't used to being alone with men, other than her brothers. It made her feel a bit uneasy—especially since this particular man was not Amish and had such an unsettling way about him.

As though he could read her thoughts, Nick said, "Don't worry, fair lady, no harm will come to you. I'm your Knight in Shining Armor. Remember that."

Miriam could feel her cheeks growing warm, but she made no reply, and she kept her face toward the window so that he would not notice.

When they pulled into a parking place at the city park, Nick rolled down his window to let in a cool evening breeze. The rain had stopped and the air felt fresh and clean. Miriam drew in a deep breath and let out a long sigh. ""Thank you for taking the time to meet me, Nick. I know that you are probably a very busy man."

Nick shrugged. "I was about to call it a day anyhow. So, tell me what has happened, fair lady. Why were you at the hospital again?"

"It is my niece Rebekah. She has been seriously injured, and it is all my fault," Miriam began, somewhat shakily.

"What exactly happened?" Nick asked, as he reached for the small notepad he had tucked inside the window visor.

At first Miriam took no notice of the fact that Nick had taken a pen from his pocket and was taking notes as she continued with her story.

"When the storm was just beginning, I sent all my students home early. I told my niece that I would give her a ride home, and I asked her to wait for me outside by the horse and buggy. I never even thought about the fact that it was parked right under a tree, or that a tree branch might break, but I—"

"A branch broke and fell on the child?" Nick asked in a very professional tone.

It was then that Miriam noticed his pen and paper. She gasped. "You are writing all this down?"

"Please go on. It's a very newsworthy item," Nick said.

"I will not go on!" Miriam shouted. "I did not call on you so that you could get a story for your newspaper column. When you offered to help before, I thought that included a listening ear."

"I have been listening," Nick said. "It's just that this is what I do. I—"

"I think you had better take me back to the hospital!" Miriam said loudly. "I can see now that this was a big mistake. Men are all alike. They can never be trusted!"

"Well, don't go getting yourself into such a huff." Nick placed the paper on the seat and put the pen back in his shirt pocket. "I won't write down another thing, Miriam. I didn't think you were going to go getting all riled up on me. I'm a reporter, so it only seemed natural to write something down that would be good as a human interest story. I'm sorry if I've offended you."

Miriam began to pull on the corner of her skirt again. She wasn't sure if she could trust his word or not. She wanted to talk, but was he really the one she should be talking to? He was, after all, nearly a stranger, and a worldly one at that.

seventeen

"Look, I can see that you really do to need to talk, and I'm more than willing to listen," Nick assured Miriam. "No more note-taking, I promise."

Miriam gave him a half-smile and nodded. "All right. As I was about to say, the tree branch broke, and it fell across Rebekah's head and back. Amos came along then, and he went to call for help."

"Amos? Who's Amos?" Nick wanted to know.

"He is the father of one of my students. Anyway," Miriam continued, "when the ambulance arrived, I rode to the hospital with Rebekah, and Amos went to tell her parents, my brother Andrew and his wife Sarah, what had happened."

"What's the child's prognosis?" Nick asked.

"Her what?"

"Prognosis. You know, her condition."

"Oh. The doctor told us that she has a concussion, and that is the reason she is still unconscious."

"That's understandable," Nick said.

"*Jah,* but he also said that there is some injury to the spinal cord," Miriam gulped, hardly able to speak the words aloud, "and that even if Rebekah does survive, she will never walk again."

"Doctors have been known to be wrong, you know," Nick said optimistically.

"I know, and I am praying for a miracle, but—"

"Oh, that's right, you Amish folks believe in all that faith stuff, don't you?" Nick asked, cutting her off.

Miriam frowned. "Faith in God is biblical, Mr. McCormick. It is not just the Amish who believe that God is in control of our lives."

"Oh, I see. I don't agree with you on something, and now

71

it's back to calling me Mr. McCormick again."

"I think I was wrong in expecting you to help me sort out my feelings," Miriam said angrily. "You are just trying to confuse me."

"Not at all, fair lady," Nick answered. "Listen, I admire you for your faith, but it's just not for me. I'm not one to put others down for their beliefs, but I don't want to rely on anyone but myself. I don't need God or faith."

Miriam sat quietly, letting his words sink in. "You must think of me as pretty old-fashioned—in appearance, as well as my ideas."

Nick reached out suddenly and took the glass of tea from her, placing it in the cup holder on the dash. He placed her hand in his and smiled. "Fair lady, I really don't want to confuse you, but I'm afraid that you have confused me."

Miriam's skin tingled underneath his touch. She had not felt this way in many years. Not since William. "How have I confused you?" she asked breathlessly.

Nick's blue eyes gleamed, and he leaned his head very close to hers. "You are so beautiful, Miriam. I find you very fascinating, yet your Amish ways are a bit strange and confusing to me. I would like to find out more about you and your Amish traditions."

"What would you like to know?"

"I know you are expected to remain separate or stand apart from the rest of the world, but I really don't understand the reasons behind such a lifestyle," Nick answered.

"The Bible tells us in Romans twelve that we must present our bodies as a living sacrifice, holy and acceptable to God. It also states that we be not conformed to this world, but rather that we be transformed by the renewing of our minds," Miriam told him. "And in Second Corinthians it says that we are not to be unequally yoked together with unbelievers. Our entire lifestyle—our dress, language, work, travel, and education are all things we must consider because of this passage in the Bible. We must not be like the rest of the world. We must live as simply and humbly as possible."

"So, things like telephones in your homes, electricity, and modern things like cars and gas-powered tractors are worldly and would cause you to be part of the world of unbelievers?" Nick asked with interest.

Miriam nodded. "The Amish community can sometimes seem harsh and uncompromising, but all baptized members are morally committed to the church and its rules."

"Hmm . . .It sounds pretty hard to live like that," Nick said, "but I suppose if you are content and feel that your way of life makes you happy, then who am I to judge it as wrong?"

Miriam was tempted to tell Nick that she was anything but happy and content, but she decided that it was not worth mentioning. Besides, if she had, then she might have had to deal with the doubts that so often swirled through her head about God and her Amish religion. She finally withdrew her hand and cleared her throat nervously.

"I really would like to help you, Miriam," Nick said earnestly.

"Just what kind of help do you have to offer?" Miriam asked.

"Well, it sounds to me like your niece is going to be in the hospital for quite a while, and she will no doubt require a lot of physical therapy and medical care."

Miriam nodded. "*Jah,* I suppose so."

"That will cost a lot of money," Nick continued.

Miriam swallowed hard. "I suppose it will."

"If I were to write an article about the girl's accident, and it gets printed in the newspaper, people will respond to it, Miriam."

"Respond? How?"

"With money, to help out with the medical bills," he answered.

"My people do not take charity from the outside world!" Miriam snapped. "We do not even believe it is right to have medical or hospital insurance. We Amish take care of each other!"

"There you go again, getting all riled up," Nick said. "I

only want to help, you know." He reached for her hand again, but she pulled it away quickly.

"I am sure that you mean well, Nick," Miriam said, "but the cost of Rebekah's medical needs is not my primary concern. Can't you understand that I am just sick about the accident? I blame myself for it, and if my niece dies, I will be accountable. Even if she survives and has to live her life as a cripple, I don't know if I can deal with it."

"Now hold on just a minute, Miriam," Nick said firmly. "There was no way that you could have known that a tree limb would fall on the child when you sent her outside. You can't go blaming yourself for something that was just a freak accident."

"But, I—" Miriam began.

Nick reached over and put a finger to her trembling lips. "You're just going to have to buck up and face this thing squarely and head on. In matters of the heart such as this, no amount of faith in God will get you through. All of us have the strength inside to battle any of the problems that life brings our way. I truly believe that."

An unbidden tear slid down Miriam's cheek. Hadn't she decided awhile back that her own determined heart was all she could count on? Perhaps Nick was right. If faith in God really was the answer, then the terrible accident would never have happened in the first place. If living a godly life was the best way, then why had God allowed Papa to die, and why had William Graber left her? Dutifully, she had served God all of her twenty-six years, and for what? To end up an old-maid schoolteacher with no father and a crippled niece to remind her that God had let her down over and over again.

Miriam looked at Nick, so obviously sure of himself, and she resolved to be done with pleading with God for His mercy and kindness. She would buck up, just as Nick suggested. She would face life head on, by herself.

She lifted her chin, and with a look of determination, said, "I think you might be right, Nick. I can face this problem head on. I'm ready to go back to the hospital now."

Nick started up the car's engine. "Please call me if you need some more advice or just want to talk. I really enjoy being with you." He reached for her hand one more time, and when she didn't pull it away, he placed a gentle kiss against her palm.

Miriam swallowed hard. Did he really enjoy being in her company, or was he just being polite? She was at a loss for words. Perhaps she would call on Nick McCormick again.

eighteen

Up at five in the morning, light the big kitchen stove, grab a jacket from the peg on the wall, head out to the chicken coop, gather eggs, slop the pigs, milk the goats. Miriam knew the routine so well that she was certain she could have done it in her sleep. It had been her routine ever since Papa died. This morning was like no other, except for the fact that the wind had picked up and it was raining slightly.

She was reminded of the day Rebekah had been injured by the falling tree limb. Could it have only happened a few weeks ago? It seemed like much longer. Perhaps that was because she kept herself so busy. Being busy seemed to help keep her from thinking too much about all of the things that had caused her heart to feel so heavy.

Rebekah was still in the hospital, but she had regained consciousness. She would live, but she would never be able to walk again. The doctors were fairly certain of that.

No matter how hard she tried, Miriam could not convince herself that she was not partially to blame for the accident. She had made up her mind that she would seek her inner strength, just as Nick McCormick had suggested. She must go on with the business of living, no matter how unhappy she was.

Today she planned to go by the hospital right after school let out. She would take some books to read to Rebekah and perhaps some of her favorite licorice candy as well. Maybe she would even call Nick from a pay phone and ask to meet him for coffee again. That thought caused her to quicken her step, as she hurried back to the house, carrying a pail of fresh goat's milk and a basket of brown eggs. Her day was just beginning, and she still had plenty of inside chores to do before she left for the schoolhouse.

❧

Not another headache! thought Miriam, as she stood at the door watching the last of her pupils leave the school yard. "Why must I always get a migraine when I have something important to do?" she said aloud. "Well, I won't let this one stop me from going into town!"

Miriam crossed the room and opened the top drawer of her desk. Inside was a bottle of Willow Bark herb capsules. She took two and washed them down with some cold water from her thermos bottle. Willow tea was used freely among the Amish for pain, and she could only hope that today the tiny capsules would work well. Was it the stress of going to the hospital or the fact that John Lapp had given her a hard time in class today that had brought on the headache? It was probably a bit of both, she admitted to herself. Determinedly, she decided not to give in to the pain or to her stressful feelings. John Lapp had been punished by losing his playtime during lunch, and she would force herself to go to the hospital, no matter how much it distressed her to see her niece lying helplessly in that bed.

❧

When Miriam arrived at the hospital, Rebekah was not in her room. She was informed by one of the nurses that the child had been taken upstairs for another CAT scan and would be back in about half an hour. Miriam could either wait in Rebekah's room or in one of the waiting rooms.

She had no desire to spend any more time than was absolutely necessary in the cramped little hospital room, so Miriam left the candy and books on Rebekah's nightstand and made her way down the hall and into the large waiting area.

Except for an elderly gentleman, the room was nearly empty. Miriam took a seat and began to thumb through a stack of magazines she found on the low table in front of her. Nothing looked very interesting, and she was just about to leave the room in search of a phone so that she could call Nick when she noticed a copy of the *Daily Express* lying on the table. *Maybe one of Nick's articles is in it*, she thought. She picked up the paper and scanned the front page. After seeing nothing by Nick McCormick, she turned to page two. She stifled a gasp. There, halfway down the page, was a picture of a young girl lying in a hospital bed. It was Rebekah, and there was a four-column story to accompany the photo.

Miriam fumed as she read the author's name—Nick McCormick, reporter. "How dare he! I hoped that I could trust him!" she hissed.

Furiously, she read the entire story, pausing only to mumble or gasp as she read how Rebekah had been struck down by a tree limb during a storm that had swept the valley. The article went on to say that the small Amish girl would never walk again and that the hospital and doctor bills would no doubt be impossible for her parents to pay. The story closed by appealing to the public's generous nature and asking for charitable contributions to the hospital on the child's behalf.

Miriam slammed the paper onto the table with such force that the elderly man seated across from her jumped. She had been hoping to see one of Nick's articles but certainly not like this! With no apologies and no explanations to the man, she stormed out of the room in search of a telephone.

There was a telephone booth down the hall, and Miriam had nearly reached it when she ran into Andrew and Sarah.

"Miriam, we didn't know you were here," Andrew said. "We dropped Simon and the baby off at Mom's, but she didn't tell us you were at the hospital."

"Mom does not know," Miriam answered. "I came right after school let out, and I—"

"You look really upset. Is there something wrong? Is it Rebekah? Is she worse?" Sarah interrupted.

"No, it's not Rebekah. She's having another CAT scan done, and I was waiting until she comes out. It's what I found in the waiting room that upset me so." She reached a shaky hand up to her forehead. Her headache, which had previously eased, was back again, this time with a vengeance.

"Miriam, you are trembling," Andrew said. "What did you

see in that room anyway?"

"A newspaper article," Miriam replied.

"The news can be quite unsettling at times," Sarah agreed. "There are so many murders, robberies, and—"

"No, no, it's nothing like that," Miriam said, cutting Sarah off. "It's a story about Rebekah."

"Rebekah?" Andrew echoed. "What do you mean?"

"The article tells all about her accident and how you will not have enough money to pay all of her medical bills. It even suggests that people donate money to help out," Miriam explained.

"What?!" Andrew said, a bit too loudly. A nearby nurse gave him a warning look, but he did not even notice.

"But who would write such a thing, and how did they know about Rebekah's accident?" Sarah asked.

"Let's go to the waiting room, and I will show you the article," Miriam suggested. She led the way back down the hall.

The newspaper was still lying on the table, where Miriam had angrily tossed it. She reached for it and handed it to Andrew. "Look here. There is even a picture of Rebekah."

"A picture? But how?" Sarah wanted to know.

"Who is responsible for all this?" Andrew snapped.

"I am afraid that I am," Miriam replied.

Andrew turned to face his sister. "You?"

She nodded. "It was I who told the reporter about Rebekah's accident, only I—"

"You called the newspaper and asked them to write an article about our daughter?" Sarah's dark eyes looked hurt and betrayed.

Miriam placed a hand on her sister-in-law's arm. "Oh, no! Please, don't think for one minute that I called the *Daily Express* or that I wanted anything like this to be printed."

"Then how did the reporter know about it?" Andrew asked impatiently.

"I think I need to begin at the beginning," Miriam said.

"*Jah,* please do," Sarah told her.

Miriam suggested that they all sit down, and then she told

them everything, except for the fact that she had nearly been taken in by Nick McCormick, even allowing herself to feel tingly and excited when he had kissed her hand. She would never admit that to anyone.

"I was on my way to the telephone to call Mr. McCormick and give him a piece of my mind when I ran into you two," Miriam concluded.

"Well, you need not worry about that task," Andrew stated flatly. "I'm going to call the newspaper office myself and demand a written apology for the article, as well as a retraction regarding the money needed. We do not want people thinking that we will take handouts from the rest of the world. We Amish stand together in times of trouble, and any help we might need will be given by our own kind!"

nineteen

The following week, a retraction on the story about Rebekah came out in the *Daily Express*. The reporter offered his apologies to all the family members he might have offended and stated that the Amish always take care of their own, so no outside help would be needed.

While it gave Miriam a sense of satisfaction that Nick McCormick had been forced to retract his story, she found that a part of her also felt sad. Not for him, but for herself. Once again, she had been let down by a man. Had she really been so naive as to believe that Nick could have been any different than other men? To think that she had nearly phoned him to ask if they might meet again for coffee and a good talk. She chided herself for being so foolish and promised not to ever allow her emotions to get in the way of good judgment again.

Rebekah had been in the hospital for nearly three weeks already, and Miriam knew that the medical bills were adding up quickly. She had a little money put aside from her teaching position, which she would give to Andrew toward the mounting bills. She also planned to sell the beautiful quilts she had made for her hope chest. Since she never planned to marry, they were useless to her now anyway. Tourists were always on the lookout for handmade quilts made by the Amish, so she would have no trouble selling them to the general store in town.

She knew several other Amish families had given money to help with Rebekah's hospital bills. How thankful she was that she belonged to a group of people who willingly helped one another in times of need. If she ever saw Nick McCormick again, she would tell him so, too!

❧

Whenever Miriam went to the hospital to visit Rebekah, she

always took a book to read, as well as some of the child's favorite licorice candy. Today was one of those days, but Miriam found herself dreading the visit. Would she ever get over the feeling of guilt she felt when she looked at the sweet, young child, lying there so helpless in her bed? Perhaps Rebekah would be asleep when she arrived, and then she could merely leave the treat and book on the table by her bed and retreat quickly back to the protection and solitude of her home.

Miriam pulled her horse and buggy to a stop in the hospital parking lot, then got out and secured the horse to a nearby post. It was beginning to rain lightly, and she hurried toward the front door of the building.

Just as she was about to step inside, Miriam collided with a man. She looked up and found herself staring into the familiar blue eyes of Nick McCormick. "You!" she cried. "How dare you show your face at this hospital again!" She stood there trembling, fighting the urge to pound her fists against her chest.

Nick smiled at her. "Miriam it's so good to see you, too. As usual, you look a bit flustered, but beautiful, nonetheless. Is there something I can do to help?"

"You unfeeling, arrogant man! You know perfectly well that just your presence here is irritating to me!" Miriam shouted.

Nick laughed lightly. "The last I heard, we were still living in a free country, fair lady. I have just as much right to be here at the hospital as you do. Or do you believe that only the Amish have the right to be here?"

Miriam clasped her hands tightly behind her back, trying to maintain control of herself. She had never been so close to striking anyone. Strangely, Nick McCormick seemed to bring out the worst in her, yet he also brought out the best.

"You know perfectly well what I mean," she told him. "The only reason you are here at all is just to be nosy and sneaky. I have no patience with a liar, Nick McCormick!"

"Excuse me?"

"Do not play innocent with me!" Miriam said loudly. "You

know very well that I am referring to the fact that you promised not to do a story about my niece. But you went ahead and did it anyway, didn't you? Your word meant absolutely nothing, didn't it?"

Nick scratched the back of his head thoughtfully and gave her a sheepish grin. "Guess I'm caught red-handed. I didn't know the Amish read the *Daily Express*."

"We are not illiterate, you know!" Miriam shouted.

"No, I'm sure you're not. That's not what I meant either," Nick said. "It's just that I thought since your religion forbids so many other worldly things, that might also include reading our worldly city newspaper."

"Never mind. I don't care in the least what you meant. I just want you to know one thing, Mr. McCormick—I am very glad that I belong to a group of people who are willing to help one another in times of need. I know that we Amish are not perfect, but we do strive for honesty, which is more than I can say for some people. And one more thing—stay away from my niece's hospital room. If you ever try going there again, I will personally report you to your superior at the *Daily Express*."

"Is that some kind of a threat?" Nick asked, trying hard not to smile.

"You may call it whatever you like."

"My, my, aren't you a little feisty thing today?" He laughed lightly. "I like spunky women—but I also like women who get their facts straight."

"What is that supposed to mean?" Miriam asked.

"Fact number one is, I never actually promised you that I would not do a story about your niece," Nick said.

"But you said—"

"That I would not do any more note-taking while you were talking to me," Nick interjected. "I kept true to my word and put away my paper and pen."

"*Jah,* but you mentioned that you would like to do an article about Rebekah's accident and the cost of her medical bills, and I explained to you that would not be necessary. The Amish—"

"I know, I know. The Amish always take care of one another," Nick interrupted. "I appreciated your input, Miriam, but I still did not promise you that I would not do a story. I did what I thought was best—as a reporter and as your friend."

"What kind of friend goes behind someone's back and does something sneaky?" Miriam asked.

"The kind that believes he's doing the right thing," Nick answered with conviction. He pulled Miriam aside and into the little waiting area that was just across the hall. "Listen, I really do care about you, fair lady. I thought I was doing something helpful for your family. I apologize if it upset you or if you thought I had betrayed you."

Miriam could feel her anger receding some. It was so hard to remain in control when she was in the presence of Nick McCormick. Did she really need to feel love and acceptance so badly that she would go outside her Amish faith to get it? She could not allow this Englishman to deceive her into believing that he could actually care for her.

"I really must be on my way now," Miriam said quickly, starting for the door. "I'm going to see my niece. I do appreciate your apology, but I would ask that you do not see Rebekah again or take any more pictures."

Nick opened his mouth to answer her, but Miriam turned away quickly and nearly ran up the hospital corridor.

Miriam found Rebekah propped up on her pillows, looking at a picture book, when she entered the room. *So innocent and sweet—and helpless*, thought Miriam.

"Aunt Miriam!" Rebekah exclaimed. She smiled happily and reached a small hand out to Miriam.

"How is my best pupil and favorite niece?" Miriam asked, as she took the child's hand.

"I feel better. My head don't—doesn't hurt no more. Doctor said I can go home soon," Rebekah replied.

Miriam cringed inside at the thought of Rebekah returning home as a cripple. Rebekah made no mention of it, however. Was it possible that she was not yet aware of the fact that she could no longer walk? How would the once-active six-year-old handle spending her days confined to a wheelchair?

"I am glad you are feeling better," Miriam said, trying to make her voice sound light and cheerful.

"Did you bring me licorice again?" Rebekah asked expectantly.

"*Jah,* and another book to read, too." Miriam handed the long licorice rope to Rebekah, then seated herself in the chair next to the bed. "Would you like me to read to you?"

"A man took my picture," Rebekah surprised her by saying.

"*Jah,* I know, but that man will never bother you again," Miriam said, and then she noticed the teddy bear sitting on the table near Rebekah's bed. She picked it up. "Where did you get this bear, Rebekah?"

"The man," Rebekah answered.

"The man? What man?"

"The picture man."

Miriam's head was beginning to pound. She reached a trembling hand to press against the side of her forehead. So Nick McCormick must have just come from Rebekah's room when she had bumped into him at the hospital entrance. Had he come out of concern for the child? Was his gift one of genuine compassion, or had he used it to bribe the child in order to take more pictures? Now that she thought about it, Nick was carrying his camera bag over one shoulder when they talked.

"Rebekah, did the man take any more pictures of you?" Miriam asked the child.

Rebekah nodded. "He gave me the teddy bear and I smiled for his camera."

twenty

Thirty days after Rebekah's accident, the doctors released her from the hospital to go home. She would still need to return to the hospital for physical therapy twice a week, but at least her days and nights could be spent with those whom she loved and felt closest to.

On Rebekah's first day home, Mom suggested that she and Miriam ride over to see if they could help out. "Sarah is really going to have her hands full now!" she exclaimed. "Just taking care of a baby and two other small children is a job in itself, but now this!"

Miriam nodded. "Since today is Saturday, and there is no school, I have all day."

"We shall hurry through our own morning chores, and then we will go right on over," Mom said.

Miriam reached for her jacket on the wall peg by the door. "I'll go out and feed the animals while you start breakfast."

A blast of cold air greeted her as she stepped out onto the back porch. It was early December, and there was a definite feeling of winter in the air.

Miriam shivered and pulled her jacket collar up around her neck. "I hate winter!" she said grimly. The truth was, she was beginning to hate all the seasons. Perhaps it was life in general that she hated. Was it all right for a believer to feel hate toward anything—even the weather? she wondered.

Then another thought entered her mind. Maybe she was not even a believer anymore. She was still Amish, but her faith in God had diminished so much over the last several years. She got little or nothing from the biweekly preaching services that she attended with her friends and family. She no longer even did her private daily devotions. Her prayers were far and few between, and then when she did pray, it was really more of a cry of complaint to God, rather than heartfelt prayers and petitions. Where was God anyway, and what had happened to her longing to seek His face?

Miriam trudged wearily toward the barn and forced her thoughts away from God and onto the tasks that lay before her.

As she returned to the house, nearly an hour later, Miriam noticed a clump of wild pansies, growing near the fence that ran parallel to the pasture. Pansies were hardy flowers, blooming almost continuously from early spring until late fall. The delicate little yellow and lavender blossoms made her think of Mary Ellen Hilty and the day that she had given her the bouquet of heartsease. *Children like Rebekah and Mary Ellen are a lot like the wild pansy*, thought Miriam. *They are small and delicate, yet able to withstand so much.*

Thoughts of Mary Ellen made Miriam think about Amos. She had seen him only twice since the day of Rebekah's accident. Both times had been at preaching services. It seemed strange that he had not come around. He hadn't even come over for supper at Mom's most recent invitation. Perhaps he had just been busy with his farm chores or taking care of Mary Ellen. Or maybe Miriam had finally made him understand that she really had no interest in him, and he had given up on his pursuit of her. Regardless of the reason, Miriam was glad that he was not coming around anymore. The last thing she needed was an unwanted suitor. Her life was already complicated enough.

She bent down and picked the colorful pansies. They would make a lovely bouquet to give to Rebekah.

⁂

Sarah was sitting on the front porch in tears when Miriam and Mom arrived. Mom quickly got down from the buggy and rushed to her side. "What is it, Sarah? Why are you sitting out here in the cold?"

"*Seind mir einge denkt in Gebeth* (Remember me in your prayers)," Sarah sobbed.

"*Jah, does Kannichdu* (Yes, I will)," Mom answered. Then, taking up the English language again, she asked, "What is the trouble?"

"I am so happy to have Rebekah home again, but there is just not enough of me to go around. Simon is into everything, the baby always seems to need me for something, and taking care of Rebekah will be a full-time job. She's only been home half a day, and I just can't manage!" Sarah sniffed and dabbed at her damp eyes with the corner of her apron.

"There, there," Mom comforted. She put an arm around her daughter-in-law's shoulder. "We will work something out."

Miriam, who had taken the buggy inside the barn, joined them on the porch. She wore a look of concern when she observed Mom comforting a very distraught Sarah. "What is wrong? Is Rebekah doing poorly?"

Mom shook her head. "Please, go inside and check on the children while I speak to Sarah."

Without any further questions, Miriam did as Mom had asked. She found Rebekah sitting in her wheelchair next to the kitchen table, coloring a picture. The child looked up and smiled. "Hi, Aunt Miriam. Do you like my picture?"

Miriam nodded. "*Jah,* it is very pretty. Rebekah, where are Simon and baby Sally?"

Rebekah pointed across the room.

Miriam gasped when she saw that three-year-old Simon had a jar of petroleum jelly and was rubbing it all over his face and hair. The baby, who was crawling on the braided rug next to Simon, had some in her hair as well.

"What in the world? How did you get this, you stinker?" Miriam said to little Simon. She reached down and grabbed the slippery jar out of his greasy hands. "This is a no-no!"

Simon's lower lip began to tremble, and tears quickly formed in the corners of his blue eyes.

"Crying will get you nowhere," Miriam scolded. "Come over to the sink with me, and let's get you all cleaned up. Then I'll tend to baby Sally."

By the time Miriam was finished with her clean-up job on both small children, Mom and Sarah had entered the kitchen. Sarah's eyes were red and swollen, but she was no longer crying.

"Our help is definitely needed here today, and there is much to be done, so let's get ourselves busy!" Mom told Miriam.

❧

By the time they reached home later that evening, Miriam was exhausted, and the last thing she wanted to do was chores, but farm chores did not wait, and so she climbed down from the buggy with a sigh of resignation, prepared to head straight for the barn.

"If you don't mind, I would like to talk before we start our chores," Mom said, as she, too, stepped down from the buggy. "Go see if Lewis is in the barn. If he is, bring him up to the house with you. The matter I have to discuss pertains to us all."

Miriam gave her mother a questioning look, but she merely nodded, then started for the barn. What could Mom have to talk about that would affect them all? she wondered.

Lewis was grooming the horses when Miriam entered the barn leading Harvey, the big dark brown horse that so often pulled her buggy wherever she needed to go. "Here is another one for you!" she called. "When you're done, Mom wants to see you up at the house as soon as possible."

Lewis looked up from his job. "What's up?"

"Mom has something to discuss, and she says that it pertains to all of us," Miriam explained.

"*Jah,* all right. Tell her I will be there in awhile," Lewis answered.

As Miriam left the barn, a chill ran through her entire body. She shivered and hurried toward the house. Was the evening air the cause of her chilliness—or was it the fear that she felt in her heart? Fear that whatever Mom had to tell them was bad news.

When Miriam entered the house, Mom had steaming cups of hot chocolate waiting, along with big hunks of Miriam's favorite gingerbread cake. Normally, Miriam would have dived right into one of the pieces of spicy cake, but tonight she did not feel particularly hungry. She just wanted to know what Mom had to say, and she knew that Mom wasn't about to tell her anything until Lewis joined them. She wished now that she had stayed to help him curry the horses. It would have gotten the job done more quickly.

"Is Lewis coming?" Mom asked, interrupting Miriam's thoughts.

Absently, Miriam reached for a slice of gingerbread and took a seat at the table. "As soon as he finishes the horses."

Mom nodded and settled herself into the rocking chair near the stove. She reached into a basket on the floor and pulled out one of Lewis's socks. It had a large hole in the heel, and Miriam wondered why Mom didn't simply throw it away.

Mom's darning needle moved in and out swiftly, as she began to make small talk. "Winter is in the air. Can you feel it?"

Miriam lifted her cup of hot chocolate to her lips. "*Jah,* I nearly froze to death this morning. I suppose I will have to get out my warm, heavy coat soon. A jacket just isn't enough for these crisp, cold mornings or evenings."

"The hens are not laying as many eggs, either," Mom continued. "That is a sure sign that winter is here."

Miriam sighed deeply. She was in no mood for small talk. What was taking Lewis so long anyway?

As though on cue, the back door opened, and Lewis entered the kitchen. "Umm. . .gingerbread! I would recognize that delicious smell if I was blindfolded and clear out on the porch!" He smiled at Mom. "Miriam says that you want to talk to us?"

Mom nodded and laid the sock aside. She cleared her throat and began. "I was wondering—that is, how would you two feel about me moving in with Andrew and Sarah? I mean, could you manage on your own?"

Neither Lewis nor Miriam spoke for several moments, then Miriam broke the silence by asking, "For how long, Mom?"

"Indefinitely," Mom answered.

"Indefinitely?" Lewis echoed.

"*Jah.* Now that Rebekah is confined to a wheelchair, and what with all the work the other two children will take—"

"But, Mom, how do you expect Lewis and me to manage here by ourselves?" Miriam asked, trying to keep her voice even.

"You are both very capable. I am sure you can manage just fine."

"I think we could do all right," Lewis said.

"That is easy for you to say!" Miriam exclaimed. "Things will not change much for you, but me—well, I will have double the work to do, and what with teaching school and all—"

"I know that my moving out will cause some discomfort for you both," Mom interrupted, "but I am badly needed over at Andrew and Sarah's."

"What about Sarah's parents? Can't they help out?" Lewis wanted to know.

"Their farm is several miles away," Mom explained. "Besides, they still have young children living at home to care for."

"It is just like you to make such a sacrifice, Mom," Lewis said. "You have such a heart of compassion."

Miriam left her seat at the table and knelt next to her mother. "It should be me that goes, Mom. I will quit my job teaching and go care for Rebekah. It was my fault that she was injured in the first place."

Mom reached out and placed a loving hand on Miriam's head. "No, it was not your fault. It was simply an accident. It was something bad that God allowed to happen. You are in no way responsible, Miriam. You are a fine teacher, and you are needed at the school. Sarah and I have already talked it over, and I have made my decision. I will be moving to their place on the weekend. I hope that I have your blessing, children."

Miriam rose to her feet. "If you are determined to go, then we shall abide by your decision."

"We will do our best to keep this place running, Mom," Lewis added.

Miriam said no more, but her private thoughts reminded her that life was not fair. There had been so many changes in the past few years, and none of them had made her happy. She lifted her chin and squared her shoulders. She would do whatever she had to in order to keep the Stoltzfus farm running. She owed Mom that much.

twenty-one

The winter months seemed to drag by unmercifully. With all the work there was to be done, the days should have passed quickly, but Miriam's tired body and saddened soul made her feel as if each day was endless. The snow lay deep on the ground, which made the outside chores even more difficult. And the cold—Miriam couldn't remember a winter that had been as cold as this one. Was it because the temperatures often dipped below zero, or was it simply because her heart had turned so cold? she wondered.

Valentine's Day was only a few weeks away, and she knew that the boys and girls at school would expect to have a party, with refreshments and exchanging valentine hearts with one another. The last thing Miriam felt like was a party, but she would force herself to get through it somehow.

Miriam found that she missed Mom terribly. She knew that her mother was doing a good thing and that her help was needed badly, but Miriam hardly ever got to see her anymore. Mom was too busy caring for Rebekah and the other two children, and Miriam had too many chores at the farm to do also. Besides, the poor weather made it difficult and time-consuming to hitch up the horse and buggy or sleigh and get out on the roads. Only for those things that were necessary, like school and church, did Miriam go out.

Lewis had begun to see a girl whose name was Grace Zepp. He'd taken her to several "singings" and more recently had begun to call on her at her home. Miriam worried about him, because ever since Papa's death, Lewis had been forced to do the work of two men. Of course, she was doing the work of two women, but she wasn't taking time out for courting. Maybe it was good that Lewis was young and obviously very much in love. How else could he have managed the extra activity of courting?

&

The schoolchildren were full of excitement on the day of the Valentine's party. Nearly everyone brought goodies. There were cookies sprinkled with red sugar crystals; cupcakes frosted in pink icing; candy hearts with silly sayings written on them; glazed, sugared, and powdered donuts; and even a big pink and white decorated cake. Miriam furnished the beverage of cold apple cider.

The party was held right after lunch and began by eating refreshments, followed by several games, and finally the children exchanged valentine cards. Some of the cards were store-bought, but most of them had been made by hand using construction paper, glue, scissors, color crayons, and in some cases even delicate white paper doilies.

Every child had taken a cardboard shoe box and decorated it, then cut a hole in the top and placed it on their school desk. They all took turns walking around the room placing their valentines into each child's special box. Miriam had instructed the class earlier in the week that each child was expected to give a card to everyone. That way no one would be left out or go home with only a handful of valentines. She even thought to make a box for Rebekah, which she placed on her own desk, reminding the children that Rebekah was unable to finish the school year because of her accident and that she would be studying at home.

Miriam felt that some valentines, a cupcake, and a few cookies would probably cheer Rebekah up, and she planned to deliver them right after school. It had been several weeks since she'd been over to Sarah and Andrew's, and she was looking forward to a much-needed visit with both Rebekah and Mom. The chores at home would just have to wait.

Miriam looked up and forced her thoughts back to the present as Mary Ellen Hilty approached her desk. The child was holding a very large valentine heart, and she handed it to Miriam with a smile. "This is for you, Teacher. It is from me and Pappy."

Miriam nodded and tried to return the smile. "*Danki,* Mary Ellen. That was very nice of you."

"And Pappy, too," Mary Ellen reminded. "He helped me make it, and he even wrote some words on it. I think Pappy likes you, Teacher."

Miriam cleared her throat and placed the valentine on her desk. "Tell your pappy I said *danki.*"

"Aren't you going to read it, Teacher?"

"*Jah,* but I will look at it later," Miriam replied. "Right now it is time for the class to begin cleaning up the room."

Mary Ellen gave her an imploring look, but she obediently returned to her seat.

Just when I thought that Amos had forgotten about me and given up, Miriam fumed inwardly.

She placed the valentine heart with a stack of papers that she would be taking home to correct, then she turned her attention back to the class.

❧

Snow was beginning to fall again as Miriam climbed into her buggy and headed for Andrew and Sarah's place. But today she did not care. She was not about to let a little snow stop her from a very overdue visit with her family.

She placed the stack of papers on the seat next to her and was about to pick up the reins, when she noticed the red and white valentine heart sticking out between two pieces of paper. "I suppose I may as well read it now," she said aloud.

On the inside, there was writing on both sides of the card. She read the left side first. It was printed and obviously done in a child's handwriting.

> *Dear Teacher,*
> *I wanted to bake you some cookies, but I do not*
> *know how to bake yet. I think you are nice and*
> *pretty, too.*
>
> > *Love,*
> > *Mary Ellen*

Miriam sighed. "I wonder just who's idea that was?" She turned her attention to the other side of the card. It was written in cursive writing.

> Dear Miriam,
>   I think of you often and wonder how you are doing. Please call on me if I can be of any help. I am praying for you and for your family.
>
>   Sincerely,
>   Amos Hilty

Miriam wiped the moisture from her cheek. Had the snowflakes drifted inside the buggy somehow? She thought all the windows were closed, but then she felt a familiar burning in the back of her throat and realized that she was crying. But why? she wondered. Surely Amos Hilty had no real concern for her well-being. He was only concerned about himself and his daughter. Was it possible that Amos did care for her, even in some small way? He had experienced the pain of losing someone close to him. He might have been sincere in expressing his desire to help.

Miriam sniffed and wiped away the tears. She needed to be loved so badly, but her heart would not let her trust any man. "I do not care if Amos Hilty is sincere," she told herself. "I care nothing for Mary Ellen's father." With a firm resolve not to think any further about the man, she picked up the reins and started down the snow-covered dirt trail that led to Andrew's place.

twenty-two

Miriam's visit with Mom, Andrew, and his family had not gone very well. The fact that Miriam was still upset over the valentine she'd received from Mary Ellen and Amos was no doubt the underlying cause, but she would never have admitted it. In fact, she chose not to even mention getting the card to anyone. Why bring questions and perhaps a hopeful comment or two?

Miriam was out of sorts when she arrived, and it took very little for a disagreement to start with her brother Andrew. The argument all began when Andrew showed some concern over the fact that snow was falling hard, and he wondered if Miriam should have driven over in the bad weather. After all, he reminded her, she was a woman who was all alone, and anything might have happened between her place and theirs. The horse could have lost its footing on the icy pavement, which would probably have caused the buggy to run off the road.

Miriam argued that just because she was a woman, it did not automatically mean that she was helpless. Then, when Andrew suggested that she needed a man in her life, she really became upset. Even Mom and Sarah got into the discussion, both agreeing with Andrew and saying that a woman Miriam's age should be happily married and starting a family of her own. Miriam told them just what she thought of that idea. Instead of staying for supper, as she planned, she went home early, not even taking the time to read a story to Rebekah.

❧

The first sign of spring came in early March, when Miriam discovered a group of little yellow crocuses poking their heads up between several clumps of grass and patches of melting snow. How she wished that the new life spring brought with it could give her a new life, too. She wanted to wake up in the morning with a feeling of joy and peace. She wanted to find a reason to begin each new day with anticipation, knowing that it truly was a day that the Lord had created and that she was going to enjoy it to the fullest.

The sound of a horse and buggy coming down the gravel drive made Miriam turn away from the flowers and look toward the buggy. She shielded her eyes against the morning sun, wondering who would be coming to call so early in the morning. She took a few steps toward the approaching buggy so that she could get a better look at the driver.

When the buggy was just a few feet away, it stopped and Amos Hilty stepped down. He smiled at Miriam and said, "Good morning. It certainly is a beautiful day, isn't it? There is a definite promise of spring in the air, isn't there?"

Miriam nodded and mumbled something about the crocuses she had just seen, then quickly she added, "What brings you out here so early in the day, Amos? There is nothing wrong with Mary Ellen, is there?" She really did feel genuine concern for the young girl, who always seemed so determined to make "Teacher" like her.

"No, Mary Ellen is fine. Since this is Saturday, and there is no school, I allowed her to spend last night with her friend, Becky Weaver."

"Oh, I see. Then if it's not about Mary Ellen—"

"I came by to see if Lewis has any horses he might like to sell," Amos interrupted. "I can use a—"

Now it was Miriam's turn to interrupt. "Horses? If you are looking for a new horse, then why not ask Henry Jost? He raises horses just for the purpose of selling, you know."

"*Jah*, I know, but I thought that maybe Lewis could use the money," Amos answered.

"We are not destitute! We do not need any of your charity either, Amos Hilty!" Miriam snapped.

"I am sorry if I've offended you," Amos said apologetically. "I don't think you need charity. It is just that with Lewis planning to get married soon, I thought he could use the extra money. I have to buy some horses anyway, and—"

"Married?! Who told you that Lewis is going to be married?" Miriam shrieked.

"He did. I thought you knew." Amos looked flustered, and he shifted nervously from one foot to the other.

"I know that Lewis has been courting Grace Zepp, but he has not said anything to me about marriage," Miriam said, trying to gain control of her voice.

"I am truly sorry. I should not have been the one to tell you," Amos apologized again. "I think maybe I have put my boot in my mouth."

"No, you were only telling me something that you thought I already knew."

"I cannot believe that Lewis hasn't told you," Amos said sympathetically.

"He probably did not want to upset me," Miriam admitted.

Amos wore a puzzled expression. "Why would it upset you if Lewis married a nice girl like Grace?"

"I have nothing against Grace Zepp," Miriam answered. "It is just that our life has been so full of changes in the last year or so. If Lewis marries Grace, it will mean more changes—especially for me."

"You mean because she will be moving into your house?" asked Amos.

"*Jah,* I suppose she will. The farm is Lewis's now that Papa is gone. And Mom is not likely to move back, either. She is needed at Andrew's." Miriam sighed deeply, then shrugged her shoulders. "The only logical thing for me to do is move out."

"But where would you go?" Amos asked.

Miriam shrugged again. "I don't know. A boarding house in town perhaps. I just know I could not stay on here. It would not be right."

"Two hens in the same henhouse? Is that it?" Amos smiled.

Miriam had to bite her lower lip to keep from smiling, too. She could almost picture in her mind Grace and her running around the kitchen, cackling and chasing each other the way that the hens in the coop often did. "No," she replied, "Grace and I would probably get on just fine together, but it would not be fair to the newlyweds to have Lewis's big sister hanging around all the time."

Amos nodded. "That is very considerate of you, Miriam. You are a good woman."

Miriam bit her lip again, only this time it was to keep from telling Amos to keep his opinions of her to himself. She felt her face turn red, and she looked away in the hopes that Amos would not notice.

"I have embarrassed you. I am sorry," Amos said quickly. He placed a large hand on Miriam's arm and drew in a deep breath. "I think I might have an answer to your problem."

"Oh?"

"*Jah.* You could marry me and move to my place. Mary Ellen loves you, and—"

"Marry you?!" Miriam's screech resounded in her own ears. "You must be joking!"

"No, I—that is—I have been thinking on this matter for some time now," Amos told her. "I will admit that I do have some serious concerns about your bitterness, and I have detected that you are not as interested in spiritual things as you should be, but—"

"Wait just a minute!" Miriam shouted. "My spiritual life is really none of your business, Amos! Besides, how would you know what I think or feel about God?"

Amos cleared his throat several times. "Miriam, I must admit that I have been watching you, and I have noted that during our church services, you often look absently out the window rather than concentrating on the sermons that are preached. You also do not participate in the singing of the Ausbund. I sense that you have become very bitter toward God. Perhaps this is because of your father's untimely death, or maybe it goes back even further to when William Graber jilted you."

"How do you know about that?" Miriam snapped.

"Miriam, this valley is not that big. There has been some talk among our people about your broken spirit and—"

"My personal life is none of your business, Amos—nor is it

the business of anyone else, either! I think this discussion had better come to a close."

Amos moved toward her, but she moved quickly away. "I am sorry if I have taken you by surprise, Miriam. I would appreciate it if you would give the matter of marrying me some deep thought and prayer. I believe that we can work through your bitterness and anger together. My only concern is for Mary Ellen. You would not let your attitude affect her, would you? I do not want my child to have any feelings of distrust toward God."

Miriam's eyes flashed angrily. "I would never do anything to hurt Mary Ellen's belief in God. She must draw her own conclusions as she matures and is dealt more of life's harsh blows. Now, regarding your proposal of marriage—you haven't said anything about love."

"I told you that Mary Ellen loves you, and—"

"*Jah,* Mary Ellen, not you," Miriam was quick to say. "You are obviously not in love with me, nor I with you. Do you not think that marriage should include love?"

Amos shifted his weight nervously and pulled on the edge of his full brown beard. "I do admire you, Miriam, and I believe that given some time, love will come—for both of us. In the meantime—"

"In the meantime, nothing!" Miriam cried. "I know exactly what you want, Amos Hilty! You want a mother for your child and someone to do all of your cooking, cleaning, and all the other wifely duties that men so desperately need!"

"No, that's not all I want. Listen, you do not have to give me your answer right now, but please, at least give the matter some thought. We can both benefit from a union in marriage."

Miriam opened her mouth as if to say something, but Amos reached out and placed two fingers against her lips. "Please say no more. We can talk again later." With that, he marched off in the direction of the barn to find Lewis.

"Men!" Miriam fumed. "They would trade their heart in exchange for a live-in housekeeper!"

twenty-three

Miriam made her way back to the house as though she was moving in slow motion. Her mind was so filled with thoughts of her conversation with Amos that her head felt like it was swimming. She wondered if he thought he would be doing her a big favor to marry her, solving the problem of where she would live after Lewis's marriage to Grace. Actually, if she were to marry him—which she wasn't—it would be her doing him the favor. After all, she was perfectly capable of finding a place to live on her own, but Amos, on the other hand, was obviously in need of a wife and mother for Mary Ellen.

She entered the kitchen and tried to focus her thoughts on what she should be doing. Baking bread and making a pot of baked beans to take to preaching service tomorrow, wasn't that what she planned to do after her walk outside? Maybe if she got busy it would help take her mind off Amos Hilty and the fact that Lewis was going to be getting married.

"How could Lewis have kept something so important from me?" she fumed, as she pulled down a tin full of flour. "Men are all alike. None of them can be trusted! I wonder who else Lewis has told, and how many other people have been hiding the truth from me. If people would talk behind my back about how William jilted me, then who knows what else they are saying?"

Miriam had her pot of beans cooking on top of the stove and four loaves of bread baking in the oven, when she heard Amos's horse and buggy finally leave. She went to the window and peered out. Sure enough, two of Lewis's horses were tied to the back of the buggy. They trotted dutifully behind.

"Humph! My guess is that he wishes he had a wife as dutiful as those horses are! *Jah*, well, it will never be me!" she exclaimed.

A short time later, Lewis entered the kitchen, carrying a broken harness. "Umm. . .something sure smells mighty good!"

"It's bread and baked beans for tomorrow," Miriam said coolly.

Lewis laid the harness on the table, then pulled out a kitchen chair and sat down. "Miriam, I think the two of us need to have a little heart-to-heart talk."

Oh, no—here it comes, thought Miriam. She pulled out a chair and took a seat across from her younger brother. "If it's about you and Grace Zepp, I already know."

"*Jah*, Amos told me that he let the cat out of the bag." Lewis smiled, then reached for Miriam's hand. "I'm really sorry you had to hear it secondhand, Miriam. I meant to tell you. I was just waiting for the right time."

"Didn't you think I could handle it? Don't you know by now that Miriam Stoltzfus can handle anything that might come her way—even disappointments?" Miriam's voice sounded harsh, even to her own ears.

"You are disappointed because Grace and I plan to be married?" Lewis seemed hurt, and he shook his head slowly. "I never expected you to be jealous, Miriam."

"Jealous? You think that I am jealous?"

"Well, yes, it does seem so," Lewis responded.

"You can't be serious, Lewis. I am not the least bit jealous."

"I just thought—"

"Well, you thought wrong! Personally, I never plan to marry, and I am not jealous of anyone who does!"

"Then why are you feeling disappointed?" Lewis asked.

"First of all, because you told Amos, who is not even a family member, before you told me, your only sister." Miriam paused for a breath, then continued. "And second, because with so many other changes, it is just a bit too much to take. First, Papa dies, then Rebekah gets injured. Next, Mom moves out of the house, and now I have to move out as well."

"No," Lewis said. "I don't expect you to move out, Miriam. This is your home, too, and I want you to stay here for as long as you like."

"I am sure that you are only saying that to be kind, Lewis. I would never dream of staying on here once you and Grace are married. It wouldn't be fair to either of you. And quite frankly, I'm not sure that I would enjoy it much, either."

"What do you mean?" asked Lewis.

"I have had complete control of the household for several months now, and another woman in the house would be a difficult adjustment. I have my ways of doing things, and I'm sure that Grace has hers as well."

"But, I'm sure that Grace would be most understanding," Lewis argued. "Besides, she will need your help."

Miriam shook her head. "For a time, but soon she will come to think of the house as hers, and she would want to run it her own way. It's only normal that she would, and I shall not stand in her way. Besides, you newlyweds will be needing your privacy. When is the big day, anyway? I need to know how long I have to get packed and moved."

"We had thought of waiting until fall, after the harvest, but Grace would like to be married in May if possible. Now that you have been told, we can be officially published at the preaching service tomorrow morning. I have already spoken to Bishop Benner, so it's just a matter of him announcing the date to the congregation."

"*Jah,* well, *Ich bins zufreide* (All right, I am satisfied). That will give me two months to find a place," Miriam answered.

"But where will you go?" Lewis asked with concern.

"I don't know yet, but there are two boarding homes in town. I will stop by one day next week and see if they have any rooms available."

"I suppose there's nothing I can say to change your mind?"

"No, nothing."

෧

The engagement and wedding date of Lewis Stoltzfus and Grace Zepp were officially published at the preaching service on Sunday, just as Lewis had planned.

On Monday, right after school let out for the day, Miriam rode into town, just as she had planned.

May Gate's Boarding House was located on a quiet street on the south side of town. It was a tall blue and white house, shaded by elm trees and surrounded by a white picket fence. It looked to Miriam like the perfect place to live. She would have solitude, seclusion, and no more farm duties or major household chores to take up so much of her time. Living in a boarding house would mean that all of her meals would be provided, and her only real responsibility would be in keeping her own room clean and tidy, and of course, teaching at the Amish schoolhouse.

Just think of all the free time I will have for reading, quilting, and visiting friends and family, she told herself, as she mounted the front steps of the big house. She could already see herself reading to Rebekah, having long chats with Mom, and spending hours getting caught up on things with her best friend Crystal. Living in a boarding home might actually have its advantages.

Since this boarding home was run by a Mennonite woman, it would be plain, but there would still be some modern conveniences, such as electricity and up-to-date plumbing. Those were things that Miriam was not accustomed to, but they were things that she could probably adjust to rather well, she decided.

Miriam rapped on the front door several times and waited patiently. Finally, an older, rather heavy-set woman, dressed in plain clothing similar to Miriam's, answered the door. "May I help you?" she asked.

"Are you May Gates?" Miriam questioned.

"I am," the woman replied.

"My name is Miriam Stoltzfus, and I'm looking for a room to rent. I will not be needing it until May, but—"

"I am very sorry, but all of my rooms are full right now, and no one plans to leave in the near future," May answered. "You might try Nora McCormick's Boarding House. It's across town, on Cherry Street."

"*Jah,* thank you, I will." Miriam turned and started down the sidewalk to her waiting horse and buggy.

"I hope you find something," May Gates called after her.

Miriam only nodded in response. She was beginning to feel a little anxious. What if the other boarding house was full, too? She hurried into her buggy, breathing a silent prayer that it wouldn't be. It was the first time she had prayed in many weeks.

Nora McCormick's Boarding House was a two-story brick house with a black wrought iron fence around it. It was colder looking than May Gate's home, but Miriam knew that she would take a room anyway, if there was one available. She rang the doorbell and waited expectantly.

A tall, slender woman of middle age answered the bell. "Good afternoon. May I help you?"

Miriam forced a smile. "Hello. My name is Miriam Stoltzfus, and I'm looking for a room to rent. I would be needing it by May."

The woman returned her smile and extended her hand. "I'm pleased to meet you, Miriam. My name is Nora McCormick. You're Amish, aren't you?"

Miriam nodded. "*Jah,* I am Amish."

"I know that you Amish are usually good, God-fearing people and would probably cause me no trouble, like some previous boarders have done, and I would truly like to offer you a room. However, all of my rooms are taken at this time."

Miriam's smile faded. "Oh, I see. Is there a chance that someone might be moving out by May?"

Nora shook her head. "That doesn't seem very likely. Most of my boarders have steady jobs in the city, and they all seem quite happy living here."

"I understand. Thank you anyway." Miriam turned to leave.

"Try May Gate's place. She's across town," Nora called.

Miriam didn't even bother to answer. What point was there in telling her that she had already been to May Gate's Boarding House and that she, too, had no vacancies? It was beginning to look as though nothing in Miriam Stoltzfus's life would ever go as planned.

twenty-four

Miriam had just reached the sidewalk by the curb, when she bumped into a man. Her mouth dropped open. "You? Why do I always keep bumping into you?"

Nick McCormick smiled and winked at her. "I guess it's just my good fortune, fair lady. It's good to see you, Miriam. I've been thinking about you and wondering how you are doing."

"I am managing," Miriam replied curtly. She didn't want to give him the impression that she needed his shoulder to cry on again. Besides, she still had not completely forgiven him for taking Rebekah's picture or for the article that he had done for the newspaper.

"You are looking very well," Nick said smoothly. "In fact, I'd say that you are more beautiful than ever. It must be springtime. It always seems to make women their loveliest."

"Are you trying to flatter me?" Miriam asked, as she felt her face turn warm.

"Not at all. I really do think you are beautiful, Miriam."

Miriam made no reply, and Nick went on. "So, what are you doing in this neck of the woods?"

"I was about to ask you the same question," she countered.

"My aunt lives here," he answered, looking up at the big brick house. "She runs a boarding house."

"*Jah,* I know. I was just asking about a room. I did not know that she was a relative of yours, however."

"If you had known, would you still have come here?" Nick said with another one of his frequent winks.

"Of course I would have," Miriam was quick to say. "I have nothing against you personally, Nick, though I know that we have had our share of misunderstandings."

"That is true, we have," Nick agreed. "But if you were living here in town, we could see more of each other, and then we'd be able to find out if we could ever see eye-to-eye on anything."

Miriam knew that her face was becoming redder by the minute, but there seemed little she could do about it. "I wish I could move into town," she said, "but unfortunately your aunt has no rooms available."

Nick frowned. "I'm sorry to hear that." He paused and shook his head. "Say, why do you need a room anyway? I thought you lived at your Amish homestead with your family."

"I do, but Mom has moved out in order to live with my older brother Andrew and his family. Andrew's Rebekah's father, remember?"

Nick nodded.

"Mom felt that her help was necessary since Rebekah is confined to a wheelchair," Miriam continued. "Then in May, my younger brother Lewis is planning to be married. He will be bringing his new bride home to our house to live. So, there is really nothing left for me to do but move out."

"You mean, they're kicking you out?"

"No, no. Lewis invited me to stay on after they are married, but I don't feel that it would be the right thing to do. Newlyweds need their privacy, and I would not really feel very comfortable having another woman come into my kitchen and perhaps begin to change things around. I'm sure that Grace will want to do things her own way, and Lewis's big sister would only be in the way."

"Have you checked at the other boarding house in town? Maybe there's a vacancy there?" Nick suggested.

Miriam shook her head. "I've already been there. I just don't know what to do. I can't really afford to pay the high rent for an apartment, and I certainly can't buy a place of my own."

Nick smiled warmly, and his blue eyes twinkled. "You could move in with me."

"Nick McCormick, you are terrible! If you know anything at all about the Amish, you should know that we do not believe in a couple living together out of wedlock!" Miriam exclaimed.

"Who says it has to be out of wedlock?" Nick asked, as he gave her another wink.

"What? What are you saying?" Miriam stammered.

"I'm saying that you can marry me," Nick answered seriously. "I'm not getting any younger, and maybe it's time I settled down with a good woman—and a beautiful one at that."

Miriam's face had grown so hot that she could feel perspiration beading up on her forehead. It was almost inconceivable that she could have had two marriage proposals in the same week—and by two men who were from opposite sides of the world, so to speak. "You are teasing me, aren't you, Nick?" she said in a near whisper.

"No, I'm not. Listen, I've surprised myself just as much as I have you by popping the question, but now that I have, I kind of like the idea," Nick said with a laugh. "The thought of coming home at night to a good home-cooked meal and a beautiful wife waiting for me is kind of appealing—even to a confirmed bachelor like me. I know we're about as different as night and day, but who knows—maybe we could make it work. We do seem to find one another easy to talk to, and it could be the adventure of our lives."

"But, but—I would have to leave the Amish faith if I were to marry an outsider," Miriam told him. "I would be excommunicated and shunned by my family and friends."

Nick reached for her hand and pulled her toward his car. "Let's go for a little ride and talk this whole thing over. I'm sure we can figure out some way to tell your folks and make them understand that it's not necessary to shun you for choosing to marry an Englishman."

Miriam's head was spinning. She felt so giddy in Nick's presence. However, there was one missing ingredient—love. She wasn't sure that the desire she felt was love. In fact, she was fairly certain that it was probably just infatuation—infatuation with something or someone that was forbidden. Still, Nick's proposal was flattering, and it did make her feel good that he would make such an offer.

"You have mentioned my beauty and how nice it would be to have home-cooked meals," she said, "but you have not mentioned anything about love. Giving up my Amish faith would be a very drastic step, with many changes to make, and I certainly could never do anything so permanent unless there was a real, lasting love involved."

Nick looked down at the sidewalk for a minute as though he were trying to collect his thoughts. "If two people are attracted to each other, as I believe that we are, then what else really matters?"

"Love," Miriam responded.

"What is love anyway?" Nick asked.

"It's trust, it's friendship, it's commitment, it's a deep longing to be together, and it's a shared feeling of great emotional depth," Miriam responded. "Do you feel those things for me?"

Nick shook his head slowly. "No, Miriam, I can't honestly say that I do, but to me, they're just not all that important. I believe that two people can be happy together if they just have a genuine physical attraction, and if they are able to have fun together. Life can be a lot of fun, you know. I don't think we need to go through life with all kinds of rules and regulations controlling us. Our government and local law enforcement does enough of that for us. Our personal lives should be fun and adventuresome."

Miriam swallowed hard. She could feel tears forming in her eyes and that familiar burning at the back of her throat. She pulled her trembling hand out of his and stepped away. "I am sure that you meant well, asking me to leave my faith and marry you, but I cannot. We hardly know each other, and even if we did, I think we both know that things could never work out between us. I have strayed from my religious teachings, and my attitude toward God has changed, but I cannot and I will not let my family down by leaving our faith for a relationship that is built on nothing more than a physical attraction between two people."

"Is that your final word?" Nick asked.

"Yes, it is," she responded firmly.

"Then you will either have to get used to living with your brother and his wife or find yourself some nice Amish man to marry. Your beauty should certainly turn some man's head. Someone who is worthy of you as his wife."

Miriam was tempted to tell him that she had just had such a proposal of marriage from Amos Hilty, but she decided against it, since nothing would be gained. She could not accept either man's proposal. There was no love offered from either Nick or Amos. And she wasn't sure that she could trust either of them. Nick had already let her down once, and Amos was only looking for a mother for his child.

"I had better be getting on home," Miriam said. "I have chores that are waiting." She walked quickly to her buggy and climbed inside.

Nick followed her, and just as she was about to pull away from the curb, he called, "I wish you only the best, Miriam Stoltzfus. If you ever change your mind about us, you know where to reach me."

Nick's final words resounded in Miriam's head for the rest of the day and on into the week that followed. Her head told her that she had done the right thing in turning down his proposal, but her heart wasn't so sure. She had to find a place to live, and marrying Nick would have been her way out. But no matter how hard she tried to rationalize such a decision as leaving the Amish faith, she simply could not give in to the temptation. The Amish culture was the only way of life she had ever known. Her security and acceptance had always come through her people. Her family and friends were important to her. She could never leave them behind, not even for love, much less a physical attraction. Love and marriage were obviously not to be for her. She had come to accept that fact, and she must learn to face life alone. But where was she going to go? She would have to work on some other plan. There had to be some adequate answer to her dilemma.

❧

Miriam sat up in bed and wiped the perspiration from her forehead. She had been dreaming. It was a strange dream about three men. First there had been William Graber, smiling and waving at her, then he drove away in his open buggy with his new bride. Then Nick McCormick came on the scene. He was following her around, with his camera pointing at her. He was laughing and calling her "fair lady." She had pulled her dark bonnet down over her face, and when she removed it again, Nick was gone, and Amos Hilty stood before her. He was holding a bouquet of heartsease pansies. What had the strange dream meant? she wondered now.

Miriam looked at the clock by her bedside and frowned. It was only four o'clock in the morning. She did not have to get up for another hour, yet she was afraid to go back to sleep. What if her dream continued? She did not want to think about William, Nick, or Amos. For that matter, it would suit her fine if she never thought of any man ever again!

twenty-five

With the month of April half over and May quickly approaching, Miriam was beginning to feel a sense of panic. She had checked the classified ads faithfully every day, and not even a single room was available for rent anywhere. She had decided that maybe she could rent or buy a place after all, but the asking price of everything within her area was just too expensive. A single woman, living on the small wages she received as a teacher, could not afford any of the high-priced places that were available.

She had just about given up and had decided that for the time being she would have to stay at the house with Lewis and Grace. She hoped that the newlyweds would understand.

One morning, on the way to school, Miriam passed Amos Hilty and Mary Ellen. They were obviously headed in the direction of the schoolhouse, too. Mary Ellen waved and smiled, calling out a cheery "Hello, Teacher!"

Miriam waved back and urged her horse into a trot. She didn't think it would be right for her students to arrive at school before their teacher did.

As she pulled into the school yard, she was relieved to see that none of the other children were there yet. She pulled her horse to a stop and climbed down from the buggy. She was just starting for the schoolhouse when the Hilty buggy entered the yard.

Miriam watched as Amos got out and went around to help his daughter down. In spite of her dislike for the man, Miriam had to admit that he was a good father, and Mary Ellen obviously loved him very much.

Just as Mary Ellen stepped down, her foot got caught in the hem of her dress. She looked down, and her lower lip began to quiver. "It is torn! My dress is torn!" she sobbed. "Pappy, please don't make me go to school today. The others will laugh at me!"

The look that Amos gave her was one of both sympathy and frustration. "I can do nothing about your dress right now, Mary Ellen. We will take it over to Maudie Miller's right after school lets out. She can mend it for you then."

Mary Ellen shook her head and gave her father an imploring look. "No, Pappy, please!"

Miriam stepped forward. "Come inside with me, Mary Ellen. I will mend your dress."

Amos gave Miriam a look of surprise. "Would you really do that for her? Do you have the necessary tools?"

Miriam gave a small laugh. "You need not be so surprised, Amos Hilty. In spite of what some may say about me, I have actually been known to do some small acts of kindness."

"I—I did not mean to say—" Amos stammered.

"Never mind, Amos. You just go on your way, and Mary Ellen will be fine." Miriam put her hand across Mary Ellen's back and guided her toward the schoolhouse, then she turned back and called to Amos, "Oh, and by the way—you do not use *tools* to sew, but I do keep a small sewing kit full of *supplies* in my desk for just such an emergency as this."

Amos mumbled something to himself and climbed back into his buggy.

Mary Ellen's face was streaked with tears, and when Miriam reached her desk, the first thing she did was to dip a clean cloth into the bucket of water that she kept nearby. Gently, she wiped the child's face. "Now stand on this chair, while I hem up your dress," Miriam instructed.

Mary Ellen gave her a questioning look.

"It would be quicker and easier if your dress was off, but some of the other children may arrive soon, and you would not want to be standing here without your dress on, now would you?"

Mary Ellen shook her head. "No, Teacher."

"Very well, then hold real still. No *rutshing* (squirming) either." Miriam quickly threaded a needle and began the task of putting Mary Ellen's hem back into place.

When the job was completed, Mary Ellen smiled happily and jumped down from the chair. "Thank you, Teacher. *Es gookt verderbt schee* (It looks mighty nice)."

"*Jah, sis gute gange* (It went well)," Miriam replied, just as the door opened and three of the Hoelwarth boys burst into the room.

Miriam was glad that the sewing job had been completed. She knew that the Hoelwarth children were all teases, and that they would have no doubt taunted and teased Mary Ellen if they had seen her standing on a chair getting her dress mended.

The morning went by quickly, and soon it was lunchtime. Miriam watched as Mary Ellen opened up her metal lunch box. The child ate hungrily, but Miriam was appalled at what Amos had given his daughter for lunch. The contents of the lunch box revealed a hard biscuit, some dried beef jerky, a green apple, and a bottle of water.

Miriam wondered if maybe Amos had just been in a hurry that morning, or was he completely ignorant as to a child's nutritional needs? Why had she never noticed before what Mary Ellen ate for lunch? Perhaps she brought lunches like this every day.

Miriam shook her head and sighed inwardly. *The man really does need a wife, and Mary Ellen certainly needs a mother!*

Miriam looked away from the child and directed her gaze out the window. She had to get her mind off of Mary Ellen and onto something else. She could feel one of her sick headaches coming on, and she had to do something to ward it off. Quickly, she reached into her desk drawer and retrieved a bottle of Willow Bark capsules. The glass of water that normally sat on her desk was half full, so she popped two capsules into her mouth and swallowed them down.

Miriam was relieved when all the children had finished their lunches and filed outside to play. Now maybe she would have a few moments of peace. But that was not to be. After only a brief time, a commotion outside ended her solitude.

When she went outside to investigate, Miriam found a group of children gathered around Mary Ellen. This was not the first time that she had witnessed some of the children picking on the child, and she wondered what the problem could be this time.

May Ellen lay crumpled on the ground, sobbing hysterically, while several of the older boys, including two of the Hoelwarths, were pointing at her and laughing. John Hoelwarth held a long stick in his hand and was poking Mary Ellen with it. "Get up, baby Hilty. Quit your crying. You are such a little crybaby!"

Angrily, Miriam grabbed the stick from John and whirled him around to face her. "Just exactly what is going on here, and why are you poking at a defenseless little girl?"

John shrugged and hung his head. "I was only trying to make her quit her bawling. She sounds like one of my pa's heifers."

All the children who stood nearby began to laugh.

"Quiet!" Miriam shouted. "I want to know why Mary Ellen was crying, and why you children have been teasing her again."

"Look at her hair, Teacher," Sara Kaiser answered. "She hasn't got a mama, and her papa can't fix it so that it stays up. She looks pretty silly."

Mary Ellen, who was still crying, had not moved from her spot on the ground.

Miriam bent down and pulled the child gently to her feet. "Come inside, Mary Ellen. I will fix your hair and clean you up." To the other children, she said, "You may all stay outside until I call you. Then we will discuss what has happened here." She turned and led Mary Ellen back to the schoolhouse.

It took nearly half an hour for Miriam to get the child calmed down, cleaned up, and her hair combed, braided, and back up into place again.

"Try not to let the children's teasing bother you, Mary Ellen," Miriam said softly. "Some of the older ones just like to make trouble. They like to pick on someone who is smaller and cannot defend themselves. They will all be made to stay after school."

"Well, *wass machts aus?* (Well, what does it matter?)" Mary Ellen said, trying to sound brave. "They will always tease me because I have no mama."

"Oh, no, I am sure that they understand that your mama died, and that—"

"If Mama was alive still, she would sew my dresses so the hems would always stay up. She would fix me good lunches like the others have, and she would do better with my hair. Pappy tries real hard, but he can't do some things the way a mama can," Mary Ellen was quick to say. She looked right into Miriam's eyes and her lower lip quivered slightly. "I wish you were my mama, Teacher."

Miriam swallowed hard. There was no doubt about it. Mary Ellen Hilty did need her. For that matter, Amos probably needed her, too. And as much as she hated to admit it, she needed them—or at least their home to live in. She knew she could never give up her faith to marry Nick, who she was very attracted to, but perhaps a marriage without love would not be such a bad thing if it did not mean she had to leave her faith and family. At least there would be mutual needs being met by all concerned.

It was a heartrending decision, but she knew now what she must do. She would speak to Amos this very day. She knew that she must tell him she would become his wife soon, before she lost her nerve.

twenty-six

"I will not tease" had been written on the blackboard one hundred times by each of the boys who had tormented Mary Ellen Hilty, and Miriam had kept the entire class after school and given them a lecture on kindness. She'd also reminded them of what the Bible teaches about doing unto others as we would have done unto us. It had become increasingly difficult for her to refer to the Bible, but she knew that it was the most appropriate lesson manual she could have used.

It had been a long, emotionally exhausting day at school, and Miriam was glad that it was finally over. Now she must ride over to the Hilty's and speak to Amos before she lost her nerve. The decision to marry him had not been an easy one, and now she had a fearful heart. Her mind was so full of questions. Would he even still want to marry her? Would Mary Ellen really be happy about it? What would her own family think? And most of all, could she really make herself go through with it?

Miriam poured herself a glass of water and swallowed the two White Willow capsules she had put in her mouth. If she was going to face Amos, it had better not be with a pounding headache. Then with a sigh of resignation, she gathered up her things and headed out the schoolhouse door to her waiting horse and buggy.

❧

Mary Ellen was sitting on the front porch, playing with a yellow and white kitten, when Miriam pulled into the yard. The child waved and ran excitedly toward Miriam when she climbed down from the buggy. "Teacher, you came to visit! Look, my hem's still in place," she said, pulling at the corner of her dress.

Miriam nodded. "I see that it is, and I see that your hair is still in place as well."

Mary Ellen smiled happily. "You did a good job, Teacher. Don't tell Pappy I said so, but you're much better at fixing hair than he is."

Miriam smiled, too. She couldn't help but like the pathetic young girl. She obviously did need a woman to care for her and to train her to do all of the feminine things that her father was unable to do. "Speaking of your pappy," Miriam said, "where is he? I need to talk to him."

"He's out in the barn," Mary Ellen answered. "I can take you there, if you want me to."

"Thank you, but I think it would be best if you stayed on the porch and played with your kitten. Your pappy and I need to talk grown-up talk for a few minutes. We will join you on the porch when we are done. How does that sound?"

Mary Ellen's eyes grew large. "You are not going to tell Pappy about those boys teasing me today, are you, Teacher?"

Miriam shook her head. "No, Mary Ellen. What I have to say to your pappy has nothing to do with the Hoelwarth boys."

Mary Ellen looked relieved, and she smiled confidently. "I'll play 'til you're done talking. Then maybe we can all have cookies and milk."

"*Jah*, maybe we can," Miriam responded. She turned toward the barn then, and Mary Ellen headed for the front porch of the house.

Miriam found Amos in a horse stall, grooming one of his buggy horses. She cleared her throat loudly so he would know she had come into the barn.

Amos looked up and smiled. "What a nice surprise! It's good to see you, Miriam. I want to thank you for mending Mary Ellen's dress this morning."

Miriam nodded. "I was glad to do it."

"What brings you out our way?" Amos asked. "Did you need to speak with me about Mary Ellen?"

"No. Actually, I came here to talk about your offer of marriage," Miriam said quickly, before she lost her nerve and decided to bolt for the door.

"Have you been thinking it over?" Amos asked.

"*Jah,* and I have," Miriam answered. "If the offer is still open, I will marry you, Amos."

Amos dropped the curry comb he was holding and took a step toward Miriam. *"Derr Herr sie gedanki!* (Thank the Lord!) I do not know what caused you to change your mind, but I am glad that you have. I think that Mary Ellen will be, also."

"Mary Ellen is the reason that I did change my mind," Miriam stated truthfully. "The child does need a woman's care. It's not that you aren't doing a fine job with her, but—"

"I think I understand what you are trying to say," Amos interrupted. "She does need a mother. She needs someone who can do all of the feminine things for her that I cannot do." He reached out and placed his hand lightly on Miriam's arm. "As you know, I do have some concerns about how your attitude might affect Mary Ellen, however."

"I would never do anything to hurt the child," Miriam was quick to say.

"*Jah,* I believe you. If there is to be a marriage, I need your word that you will not let your bitterness show to Mary Ellen. You must help me train her in God's ways, and you must set a good example for my daughter."

Miriam pulled away from his touch. She was beginning to wonder if she had done the right thing after all. Could she really keep from letting her bitter heart be noticeable to Mary Ellen? Could she set the child a good example?

Amos smiled and said softly, "I, too, need you, Miriam. I need a wife."

"Do you mean just for cooking and cleaning, or in every way?" Miriam asked boldly.

Amos shuffled his feet and looked down at the dirt floor of the barn. His face had turned slightly red, and he stammered, "I—that is—I would like a loving, physical relationship with my wife, but if you do not feel ready—"

"I am not ready!" Miriam stated, a little too harshly. "I may never be ready for that, Amos. If this will be a problem for you, then perhaps we should forget the whole idea of marriage."

"No, no. I will wait patiently, until you feel ready for my physical touch," he answered. "Until then, we will live together as friends and learn about one another. Maybe as our friendship grows, things will change between us."

"I do not want to give you any false hope, Amos. I do not think that I can ever love you," Miriam told him as gently as she knew how.

"We shall see," Amos said. "And now, let us go up to the house and tell Mary Ellen our news. I'm sure that she will be delighted."

So it was decided, just that simply. Miriam could hardly believe that Amos had accepted her conditions. *He must really be desperate for a housekeeper and a mother for his child*, she reasoned. *Of course, I had to agree to his conditions as well.*

Mary Ellen was still on the porch playing with her kitten when Amos and Miriam joined her. She looked up at them expectantly. "Can we have some cookies and milk, Pappy?"

Amos smiled down at his daughter. "That sounds like a fine idea. Let's go inside. We will sit around the kitchen table, eat our cookies, and talk. Miriam and I have something very important that we want to tell you." Mary Ellen reached for her father's hand, and they all entered the house.

It was the first time Miriam had ever been inside the Hilty house. Amos never opened it up for Sunday services, and it was obvious to her why he didn't. The house wasn't really dirty, just very cluttered and unkempt looking. If there had ever been any doubt in her mind about whether Amos needed a wife or not, it was erased now. The touch of a woman in the house was greatly needed.

Amos poured tall glasses of fresh milk, while Mary Ellen went to the cookie jar and got out some cookies that were obviously store-bought. When they had all taken seats at the table, Amos cleared his throat loudly and said, "Mary Ellen, how would you like it if Pappy got married again?"

Mary Ellen looked at him questioningly. "A new mama for me?"

Amos smiled and nodded. "A wife for me and a mama for you."

Mary Ellen turned to face Miriam. "Is it you, Teacher? Are you going to marry Pappy?"

"How would you feel about that, Mary Ellen?" Miriam asked.

Mary Ellen smiled, a smile that reached from ear to ear. She reached out and took hold of one of Miriam's hands. "I would like it very much. When can you come to live with us?"

Amos laughed. "Not until we are married, little one."

"When will that be?" Mary Ellen wanted to know.

Amos looked at Miriam, and she shrugged. "As soon as possible, I suppose."

Amos nodded in agreement. "I will speak to Bishop Benner right away. I will ask that we be published at the next preaching service."

"Maybe we could be married on the same day as Lewis and Grace," Miriam suggested. "We would be inviting pretty much the same people anyway, and if we have a double wedding, it will keep the cost of the food and everything down."

"That is a fine idea," Amos answered. "Would you like to speak to Lewis and Grace about it?"

Miriam reached for a cookie. "*Jah,* I will talk to them tonight."

twenty-seven

The date of Lewis and Grace's wedding had been set for the second Saturday of May. They were both overjoyed at Miriam's announcement that she was going to marry Amos Hilty, and they happily agreed to share their wedding day with them.

Mom was happier about the news of her daughter's wedding than anyone. Noting that they had only a few weeks, she quickly set about sewing a simple wedding dress for Miriam to wear. Miriam didn't want any fuss made, and she would have just as soon been married in one of the dresses she already owned, but Mom wouldn't hear of it. She insisted that all brides must have a new dress for their wedding day.

Miriam was certain that Mom and nearly everyone else in the family thought she was marrying Amos because she had changed her mind about him, and perhaps that she even now loved him; she had no intention of telling them anything otherwise. However, Miriam knew that Crystal, whom she had not yet told, would not be so easily deceived.

Crystal stopped by to see Miriam the day after she had already told the rest of the family. Crystal had left the twins with a neighbor and was planning to ask Miriam if she would go into town to do some shopping.

"I really don't feel much like shopping today," Miriam told Crystal, "but thank you for thinking of me."

"Do you have some other plans for the day?" Crystal asked.

"No, not really. Just the usual work around here," Miriam answered.

"Then let's get out for a while. It will do us both good. Besides, you stay around here working far too much," Crystal argued.

Silence filled the room as Miriam sat on the edge of her

kitchen chair, blinking back the tears that had suddenly gathered in her eyes. She felt Crystal's arm encircle her shoulders.

"What is it, Miriam?" Crystal asked with obvious concern.

"Amos Hilty has asked me to marry him."

Crystal gasped. "Really? When?"

"Several weeks ago, but yesterday I gave him my answer."

"And what was your answer?" Crystal asked.

"I told him that I would marry him," Miriam said with a catch in her voice. "I know that he does not love me, Crystal. He only wants a housekeeper and a mother for Mary Ellen."

"Then why did you accept his proposal?"

"Mary Ellen needs me," Miriam stated flatly. "I know that I have said many times that I would never marry without love, but there will be love, Crystal. Mary Ellen's love for me, and my love for her."

Crystal took a seat across from Miriam. "I sense that you have some doubts."

Miriam nodded. "*Jah.*" She wiped the tears from her face with the back of her hand. "Part of it is the fact that there is no love between Amos and me, but my main concern is trust. I don't know if I can trust Amos."

"Trust him how?" Crystal asked.

"He has agreed not to force a physical relationship on me, but men are all alike," Miriam said. "Men are selfish, and—"

"Miriam, all men are not like William Graber," Crystal interrupted. "Amos Hilty appears to be a very honest man. I do not believe that he will hurt you the way that William did. However, since you obviously feel no love for him, and you say he does not love you, either—"

"He does not!" Miriam exclaimed.

"Then maybe it would be best if you do not make a life-long commitment to him," Crystal told her. "Divorce is not an acceptable option among the Old Order Amish, as you know."

"So you are saying that I should call the marriage off?"

"I am only saying that I feel you need to give the matter much prayer and thought," Crystal answered. "I want to see you happy, and if you marry someone whom you feel no love for, how can you ever be truly happy?"

Miriam shrugged. "I have found that life is not always happy."

"Until you get rid of your feelings of mistrust and allow God to fill your heart with love and peace, you will never be happy, Miriam."

"I have learned to manage without love or happiness," Miriam replied. "Besides, if I do marry Amos, it will benefit all three of us. I won't be living here with Lewis and Grace, so they will be much happier. Mary Ellen will have a mother to care for her needs properly. And Amos will have someone to cook and clean for him."

"And what about your needs, Miriam?"

"I will be well taken care of—a roof over my head, a hard-working husband, and a child to love." Miriam paused. "I do have some serious doubts about all this, but I believe that I must go through with it. I hope that as my very best friend, you will support me in this decision. I would like you to be one of my attendants, if you are willing."

"Of course I am," Crystal assured her. "I will help with your wedding plans in any way that I can. If you are doing what you feel your heart is telling you to do, then I will support you with my love and my prayers."

Miriam stared at the table in front of her. "I am not thinking with my heart, only my head. My common sense tells me that this is the right thing to do."

❧

With only a week before the wedding, Miriam found that she still had several things to buy in town. She was beginning to wish that she had taken Crystal up on her offer to go shopping the Saturday before. "I will just have to go alone today," Miriam told herself. "It's the last Saturday before the wedding, so I really have no other choice." As soon as her chores were done for the morning, she hitched up her horse and buggy and started for town.

The Country Store, her favorite place to shop, was unusually busy. Not only were there many Amish customers, but there were also a lot of tourists. Miriam disliked crowds, especially when she knew that the tourists would be watching her and all the other Amish who so often shopped in the little rural town. If these English people had been merely shopping, then most of them would have gone into the big city of Lancaster.

Miriam moved to the back of the store, where the household items were. There was an oil lamp on one of the high shelves that she wished to look at, but it was too high for her to reach. She looked around for the store clerk, but he was not in sight. She sighed and turned away, deciding to look at some material instead.

"Do you need some help?"

Thinking that perhaps one of the other clerks had come to her aid, Miriam turned back and said, "*Jah,* I would like to see—" Her mouth fell open. "Nick McCormick! What are you doing here?"

Nick smiled his usual heart-melting smile. "I like to come here on weekends. I get lots of story ideas from watching the people."

"You mean *my people,* don't you?" Miriam was quick to say.

Nick gave her a playful wink. "The Amish are very interesting people. Especially you, fair lady. I find you to be the most fascinating Amish woman of all."

Miriam's cheeks grew warm. Why did Nick McCormick have such a way about him? she wondered. She knew that she was considered quite plain by her own people, but in Nick's presence she actually could begin to believe that she was pretty.

"You know, I think it must be fate, us always running into each other. Maybe we really are meant to be together, Miriam," Nick said, as he leaned his head very close to hers.

Miriam quickly pulled away. What if someone she knew saw her engaged in such a personal conversation with this Englishman? "We are not meant to be together, Nick."

"Your lips say so, but your eyes tell me something different," Nick whispered.

Miriam felt her hands become clammy and her heart was beating fast against her chest. She had to get away from Nick McCormick as quickly as possible. Yet she did not want to leave the store until she had completed her shopping. "If you will excuse me, I really must find a clerk to help me."

"What kind of help do you need, fair lady?" he asked smoothly.

She looked overhead at the shelf above. "I need some help getting that kerosene lamp down."

"No problem at all," Nick said. He reached for the lamp and handed it easily down to Miriam. "Here you are."

"Thank you," she replied.

"So, how are things with you these days?" Nick asked. "Did you ever find a room to rent?"

Miriam shook her head. "No. I no longer have any need of a room."

"Oh? And why is that?"

"I am getting married in a week," Miriam stated.

Nick frowned. "I see. So, who's the lucky fellow?"

"He is a very nice Amish man," Miriam answered.

"I didn't think he'd be anything but Amish," Nick countered. "I know that a girl like you could never be truly happy with someone like me, who's an outsider. You were right to turn my offer of marriage down. We both know that it probably would never have worked out for us."

Miriam was tempted to tell him that she wasn't going to be happy with Amos, either, but instead she just nodded and said, "You are right, of course. I could never be happy with someone who wasn't Amish."

Nick leaned in close to her ear and whispered, "I would ask for a kiss from the bride-to-be, but I suppose just a word of congratulations would be more appropriate under the circumstances." He smiled. "Listen, I'd like to do something for you, if you'll let me."

"What is it?" Miriam asked hesitantly.

"Let me buy that oil lamp for you. It will be my wedding present to you. Whenever you look it, maybe you'll remember me and know that I am happy that you have found someone to love you."

Miriam swallowed against the lump that had formed in her throat. How could Nick know that she had not found someone to love her—except for Mary Ellen, that is.

"Please, don't deny me this pleasure?" Nick coaxed. "It would make me very happy."

Miriam shrugged. "*Jah,* I suppose it will be all right." Who was she to stand in the way of anyone's happiness?

twenty-eight

As Miriam's wedding day approached, she found herself feeling more and more anxious. She wondered at times if she could really make herself go through with it, but then she would remind herself that she really did need another place to live and that Mary Ellen desperately needed her. With those thoughts in mind, she determined in her heart to follow through with the commitment she had made to Amos.

On the day of the wedding, Miriam awoke with a headache. "Oh, no!" she groaned. "Not today!" She forced herself to get dressed and headed downstairs to the kitchen.

As she sat at the table drinking the cup of peppermint herb tea she had used to wash down two White Willow capsules, she began to reflect on her life. She rubbed her forehead thoughtfully and thought about the only life she had ever known. Here at this familiar old house, all of her memories swirled around in her head. She had been born here. Right upstairs in Mom and Papa's room. She had grown up here. She'd never known any other home. Now everything had changed. Papa was dead, Mom was gone, moved in with Andrew and Sarah, and she and her youngest brother Lewis were both about to be married. She would be moving away to Amos Hilty's house, where she would be his housekeeper and Mary Ellen's new mama. Lewis would be bringing a new bride to Miriam's home, and she would soon be its new mistress. Nothing would ever be the same again.

She swallowed hard, trying to force that old familiar lump out of her throat. Her eyes stung with the threatening tears. She didn't belong here anymore, but oh, how she would miss this home.

"Good morning, bride-to-be!"

Miriam turned and saw Lewis standing in the doorway,

smiling from ear to ear.

Does he actually think that my heart is happy this morning? she wondered. "Good morning, groom-to-be," she answered, instead of voicing her true thoughts.

"This is our big day, Sis. Are you feeling a bit anxious?"

Miriam nodded. "*Jah,* just a bit. And you?"

Lewis smiled. "I would be lying if I said I wasn't, but my heart is so happy that I feel like it could burst at any moment!"

"Grace is a wonderful girl," Miriam told him. "I am sure that the two of you will be very happy living here together."

"*Jah.* I hope we can be as happy as Mom and Papa were for so many years. I am very happy for you and Amos, too, Miriam," Lewis added. "You both deserve some real joy in your lives."

Miriam groaned inwardly, but outwardly she managed a weak smile. She was glad that her brother's heart was so happy. She only wished that she could feel more than an anxious heart on the morning of her wedding day.

❧

The three-hour wedding ceremony began at nine o'clock in the morning and was similar to a Sunday morning preaching service. It was held at the home of Grace's parents, since their house was larger than the Stoltzfus home and could accommodate more guests.

Both brides, dressed in plain blue cotton dresses draped with contrasting capes and aprons, and wearing black prayer caps on their heads, appeared to be quite anxious. However, this anxiousness was for quite different reasons. Grace was anxious and excited to become Lewis's bride, while Miriam was anxious and nervous about becoming Amos's bride.

Grace had asked her sister Martha and a friend named Faith to be her attendants, and Miriam had chosen Crystal and Sarah as hers.

Lewis and Amos both wore white shirts, black trousers, and matching vests and jackets. They also had on their heads black hats with three-and-a-half inch brims.

Jonas and Andrew were Lewis's attendants, and Amos had

asked two Amish men named Joseph and Philip.

The wedding included the congregational singing of several hymns from the Amish hymnbook called the *Ausbund*, a long sermon on the subject of marriage, with Scripture references taken from both the Old and New Testament, testimonies from several of the church leaders, a time of counseling in another part of the house for the brides and grooms, an extended prayer, and of course the traditional wedding vows.

The vows were the part of the ceremony that Miriam had dreaded the most, knowing that both men and women of the Amish faith take their wedding vows very seriously. Divorce would not be an acceptable option if things did not go well between her and Amos. The bride and groom were expected to work out their problems, and above all else, remain true to the vows that they had spoken before God and man.

Though Miriam's intent was to remain married to Amos Hilty until death would part them, it was not going to be easy to promise to love, honor, or obey. She might be able to honor him, and if his demands were not too great, possibly she could obey him—but love? She knew that was out of the question. She would never feel anything more than perhaps a mutual respect for Amos. She hated the idea of reciting her vows and not really meaning them, but what other choice did she have? she reasoned. She was doing the right thing for Mary Ellen, and no one but her and Amos would know this was not to be a marriage based on love.

Miriam tried to push the guilt that she was feeling aside as she took her place beside her groom. They were the older of the two couples being married, so they would repeat their vows before the bishop first.

Miriam thought that if Bishop Benner had only known about her lack of faith in God and the circumstances of her marriage to Amos, he probably would not have agreed to perform the ceremony until Miriam had come to see the error of her ways. She was glad that the man could not see into her heart and know what she was really feeling.

When the vows had been said, the bishop blessed them and

they sat down again. Miriam swallowed hard. It was done. There was no going back now. She was Mrs. Amos Hilty and would remain so until the day that either she or Amos died.

Amos had taken her hand as they found their way back to their seats on the backless benches. She had not resisted, since they were in full view of all the nearly two hundred guests. There had been no traditional wedding kiss, as most people outside of the Amish faith usually exchange when they become husband and wife. Kissing and other such demonstrations of affection were to be kept for private moments, when the bride and groom were alone. Only both Amos and Miriam knew this was not to be the case in their own marriage. It was a marriage of convenience, not of love or even physical attraction. While Amos was not hard to look at, he certainly did not hold the appeal for Miriam that Nick McCormick had.

Now it was the younger couple's turn to stand before the bishop and say their vows. Grace smiled shyly yet happily up at her groom, and the love that she obviously felt for him could be seen by all. Lewis returned her smile, and his face, too, showed love for the woman who was about to become his wife.

As Miriam watched, her eyes misted. She felt joy for her younger brother and his bride, but a heavy heart for herself. She would never know a love such as theirs. She was now a married woman and would wear a white head covering from now on, but her heart would always be empty and pained.

twenty-nine

When the final prayer had been said by the bishop, the wedding service was officially over. Everyone filed outside to wait for the meal to be served. Since there were more guests than indoor seating, groups of people took turns filing into the house to eat. Both brides and grooms were seated at a special table called the *Eck,* because it is in the corner. From their vantage place, the young couples could see all their guests and be free to visit while they ate the sumptuous wedding meal. There were platters full of fried chicken, roast beef, and ham, accompanied by large bowls of mashed potatoes, stuffing, several kinds of vegetables, coleslaw, and numerous relish trays. Coffee, tea, milk, and apple cider were also available as beverages. For dessert, there was cherry pie, donuts, fruit salad, tapioca pudding, chocolate cake, and homemade ice cream. Miriam ate until she couldn't swallow another bite. Everything tasted so good.

Mary Ellen, who was sitting next to her, smiled and said, "Can I call you Mama Mim now, Teacher?"

Miriam laughed lightly. "*Jah,* if you like, but only at home. You must still call me Teacher when you are at school."

"You mean you will be my mama and my teacher, too?" Mary Ellen asked.

"Of course I will," Miriam began.

"Now that is something that Miriam and I will need to discuss later on," Amos said.

Miriam wanted to tell him that there was nothing to discuss, but rather than cause a possible scene, she merely smiled and patted Mary Ellen's hand. "Why don't you run along outside and play with some of your friends?"

The child moved closer to Miriam's side and whispered, "I would much rather stay with you, Teacher—I mean, Mama Mim."

Instead of a honeymoon, most newlywed Amish couples spend their weekends visiting their extended families in order to receive gifts so that they may set up housekeeping in the proper manner. Due to the fact that Amos already had a fully stocked home, he did not feel that it was necessary to receive any gifts, so he and Miriam would not be spending their weekends anywhere but in their own home.

Miriam argued, saying that Lewis and Grace were also living in a fully stocked house, and that they were planning to follow the traditional Amish custom of visiting and collecting gifts. When this statement did nothing to change Amos's mind, she tried another tactic. "Amos, we really could use a few things to make our home a bit more comfortable, such as some new blankets and quilts, perhaps some braided rugs—and even the food supply in your pantry is rather low."

"I will give you the money to buy whatever you think is needed," Amos told her firmly, making it quite clear that the subject was closed.

So this is how it is going to be, thought Miriam, as she cleared away the breakfast dishes. *No wonder he could not find another wife.*

Miriam had only moved into Amos's house the day before, and already she wondered if she had made the biggest mistake of her life. Since today was an off Sunday, and there would be no regular preaching services, she and Amos could use the time to get a few things straight between them. Once the morning chores were finished, they should be able to talk without any interruptions.

Mary Ellen, who was playing on the kitchen floor with her kitten, looked up at Miriam and smiled. "I'm so glad you have come to live with Pappy and me."

Miriam smiled back but said nothing. How could she explain to the small child that she herself was anything but glad about the arrangement? Had it not been for Mary Ellen, she would probably not be standing in Amos's kitchen right now.

Amos pushed his chair away from the table and stood up.

He walked across the room to the stove and removed the coffee pot. "Mary Ellen, would you please take your kitten and go outside for a while?"

Mary Ellen looked at her father with questioning eyes. "You and Mama Mim want to be alone, don't you, Pappy?"

If only that were true, thought Miriam. The last thing she wanted was to be alone with her new husband.

"Miriam and I need to talk," Amos told his daughter. "It is a beautiful spring day, and if you go outside to play right now, later, after the chores, we will all go on a picnic at the lake."

"Really, Pappy? I love picnics!" Mary Ellen scooped the fluffy kitten into her arms and bounded out the back door.

Amos put the coffee pot on the table and pulled out a chair for Miriam. "Please, sit down once."

"But I have dishes to do," Miriam argued.

"The dishes can wait. We do need to talk," he told her.

Miriam dried her hands on a towel and took the seat he had offered her. She knew he was right. They did need to talk, and she supposed now was as good a time as any.

Amos poured them both a cup of coffee and sat down across from Miriam. "I believe that God has brought us together, Miriam. I also believe that He will bless our marriage. *Wass Got tuht ist wohl getahn* (What God doeth is well done). However, there are many adjustments that need to be made, and some of them will take some getting used to."

Miriam nodded and blew on her hot coffee. She did not voice the thought, but she certainly did not believe that God had anything to do with them being together. It was a mutual decision, made by two consenting adults, because they both needed something that the other could give.

"I believe strongly, as do most Amish men," he continued, "that the man is to be the head of the house. The Bible confirms this fact in Ephesians chapter five, verse twenty-three, where it says, 'For the husband is the head of the wife, even as Christ is the head of the church.' Therefore, while I may consult you on certain important matters, I feel that the final decisions must be made by me."

Miriam looked up from her coffee and stared directly into his dark brown eyes. "Are you saying that I must do all that you say?"

Amos reached for her hand, but she quickly withdrew it. "You promised that this would not have to be a physical union!" she shouted. "Are you not a man of your word, Amos Hilty?"

Amos stood up and began pacing the floor. "I will be true to my promise, Miriam. I will not touch you unless you ask me to. I will continue to sleep alone, just as I did last night."

Miriam thought about the night before, her wedding night. It had not been at all the way she had always dreamed of it being. After tucking Mary Ellen into her own bed, Miriam had left the child's room and slipped quietly into the bedroom across the hall. The room had previously been used for guests. Amos's room was right next to hers, and she could hear him moving about in it. She had lain awake most of the night, worrying that he might change his mind and come to her room. He had been true to his word then, but when he touched her just now, she had been greatly troubled and full of new doubts about whether he could be trusted.

"It is about other matters that I must have the final say," Amos said, interrupting Miriam's private thoughts.

"What matters are you referring to?" she asked.

He took a seat at the table again and drank some coffee before answering. "First of all, there is the matter of you continuing to teach at the school."

"What? But I thought you understood just how important teaching is to me. It's been the most important thing in my life, and—"

"I understand that, Miriam, but now you have a new life here with me and Mary Ellen. You have new responsibilities. Mary Ellen needs a full-time mother."

"I can be her mother and still be her teacher!" Miriam said loudly.

"It would never work," Amos stated emphatically. "There are many things which need to be done here at home, and if you worked—"

"I could do my chores here and still teach," Miriam interrupted. "I have been doing it for several years at home."

"But you did not have a child to care for," Amos reminded her. "Also, there is the matter of how the children at school would react to having one of the other students' mothers as their teacher. They might feel that you would show favoritism toward Mary Ellen."

"I would never do that!" Miriam was quick to defend.

"Perhaps not intentionally, but some might believe you were anyway."

"But the school year is nearly over," Miriam argued. "There are only a few weeks left, and it would be difficult to find a replacement on such short notice."

Amos nodded. "You are right. I will make one concession then. You are free to continue teaching for the rest of the school term, but the elders will meet and hire another teacher for next fall's term. I believe that I can convince them to let you stay on until then. It is not customary for us to allow married women to be the schoolteacher for our children, you know."

As though the matter was entirely settled, Amos stood up, crossed the room, removed his straw hat from the wall peg, placed it on his head, and started out the back door. He turned back just before he closed the door and said, "Do not forget about our picnic at the lake. Some fried chicken would be very nice. It is Mary Ellen's favorite."

Miriam stuck out her tongue at his retreating form. "What in the world have I gotten myself into?" she moaned.

thirty

A routine was quickly established at the Hilty home, and Miriam found herself adapting to it, but she didn't think she could ever adapt to being a wife. Her heart longed for something more than wifely chores to do. Being a stepmother to Mary Ellen helped to fill a part of her that seemed to be missing, but there was still something else that she longed for. She didn't want to admit it, not even to herself, but she longed for the love of a man. She found Amos's presence and often his gentleness to be unnerving. It made her keenly aware of the great emptiness in her life. In the past she had managed to keep her life fairly uncomplicated because she had forgotten what love felt like. But now she had the strange sensation, a need really, to love and to be loved. Longing for love did not bring love into one's life, though, so she told herself that the best thing she could do was to keep busy. She was certainly doing a good job of that.

One evening after supper, Amos picked up his Bible to read, just as he did every night. At first, Miriam had been irritated by the practice, since she had long ago given up reading her own Bible every day. But now she found herself able to tolerate the ritual he had established. It was a time when the three of them sat around the kitchen table, reading God's Word as a family, and then taking the time to talk about what they had read. Mary Ellen usually had questions, and Amos seemed to take great pleasure in being able to interpret the Scriptures for his daughter.

"Tonight we will be reading in Proverbs," Amos said, as he opened the Bible. " 'Whoso findeth a wife, findeth a good thing, and obtaineth favour of the Lord.' " He looked up and smiled. "That was chapter eighteen, verse twenty-two."

Mary Ellen reached over and pulled on her father's shirt

sleeve. "Mama Mim is a good wife, isn't she, Pappy?"

"*Jah,* she is," Amos answered, as he looked right at Miriam.

His gaze made her feel uncomfortable, and she quickly looked away. Her slim fingers were so tightly clenched around her coffee cup that the veins on her hands stuck out.

"Is there more in the Bible about Mama Mim?" Mary Ellen asked.

"Let's see," Amos said, as he began thumbing through the pages. "*Jah,* here in Proverbs thirty-one, verse twenty-seven, it says, 'She looketh well to the ways of her household, and eateth not the bread of idleness.' "

Mary Ellen gasped. "Pappy, you mean that Mama Mim is not supposed to eat any bread? Won't she get awfully hungry?"

Amos laughed, and even Miriam did as well. It felt so good to laugh. It was something that she did so seldom.

Mary Ellen was looking up at her father, her hazel eyes large and expectant. Amos reached out and patted her head. "The Bible verse is not talking about real bread, Mary Ellen. The bread of idleness refers to someone who is lazy and does not work much."

Mary Ellen frowned. "But, Mama Mim works all of the time. She works at school, and she works here, too. She is always busy doing something."

Amos nodded. "I know she is. In fact, that verse is saying that a good wife is not idle or lazy, and it is speaking about someone just like Mama Mim. She looks well to our house, and that means she takes good care of us. She does not eat the bread of idleness, which means that she is not lazy."

Mary Ellen smiled and took both her father's hand and Miriam's hand. "I am so glad we have Mama Mim."

Amos looked at Mary Ellen and then at Miriam and smiled. "*Jah,* I, too, am glad."

❧

The last day of school was June sixteenth. The children were all excited, as they were about to begin their summer break, even though it meant that many of the older ones would have a lot more chores to do at home.

Miriam found herself feeling moody and depressed. This was to be her last day of teaching. She would not be returning in the fall, as she had for the past several years.

She reached into her desk drawer for some White Willow capsules, feeling as though one of her headaches was coming on. She'd had a lot of sick headaches during her days of schoolteaching, she realized. Maybe once she quit, the headaches would be gone as well. Maybe staying at home and doing domestic chores all day would be less stressful.

Another thought occurred to Miriam. Amos was a farmer, and he would be in and out of the house throughout the day. She would be forced to see him more often. She was thankful that at least Mary Ellen would be there all summer long. The child would keep her busy and give her an excuse to avoid too many conversations with Amos.

She glanced at the clock and realized that it was almost time to dismiss the class. She swallowed the lump in her throat and tried to think about something else. What she really needed was a long overdue visit with Mom. She always seemed to understand her and was usually full of good advice, even if Miriam often chose not to take it.

Just before Miriam dismissed the class that afternoon, she told them that she had an announcement to make. "Today was my last day of teaching," she said, trying to make her voice sound calm and steady. "I will not be returning in the fall."

"You mean we will have another teacher?" John Hoelwarth asked, without raising his hand.

Miriam nodded. "*Jah,* that is right, John."

"Teacher is my mama now. That is why she is not coming back," Mary Ellen spoke up. "She will be too busy to teach. She has to take care of me and Pappy."

The class fell silent, and Miriam stood up and moved away from her desk. "I have enjoyed being your schoolteacher, and I will miss you all."

"I won't miss her," John Hoelwarth whispered to the boy in front of him. "I think she is mean, and she hardly ever smiles."

Andrew Sepler nodded and whispered back, "*Jah,* she has a

heart of stone, all right."

Miriam frowned at the boys. "Do you two have something that you wish to share with the rest of the class?"

Andrew quickly shook his head. "No, Teacher."

"Very well, then stop your whispering."

Both boys sat up straight and became quiet. Neither of them wanted to be kept after school on their last day before summer break.

Miriam looked up at the clock on the wall. "It is nearly time to go. If you will all clear out your desks, you may be dismissed a few minutes early."

Everyone hurried to do as their teacher had instructed, then one by one, they all filed out the door, laughing and calling to one another as they entered the school yard. Everyone except for Mary Ellen. She came to stand by Miriam. "I like riding home with you, Mama Mim," she said. "Pappy doesn't have to come and get me anymore." She frowned. "What about next year, when you are not my teacher? How will I get home then?"

"You will either walk with some of the older children, or I will come and pick you up. On very cold, rainy, or snowy days, you will need a ride home," Miriam answered. She turned to gather up the last of her things, and as she started toward the door, she turned and looked back, letting her eyes travel around the entire schoolroom. She swallowed the irritating lump and stepped outside with Mary Ellen right at her side.

❧

Miriam found that no matter how busy she kept herself, the feelings and longing in her heart did not go away. In fact, the longer she lived under Amos's roof, the more they were intensified.

One day, while visiting with Mom, she was told that her newest sister-in-law, Grace, was in a family way.

"That is wonderful," Miriam told her mother, trying to sound as excited as possible. "I am very happy for Lewis and Grace."

"And what about you, Daughter? When are you going to start your family?" Mom asked suddenly.

Miriam poured herself another glass of lemonade, then replied, "I already have a family. Mary Ellen is a good child, and—"

"*Jah,* I am sure that she is, but wouldn't you like a baby of your own?"

Miriam's eyes flooded with tears, and she quickly looked away so that Mom would not notice. How could she explain to her mother that her heart did long for a baby, but that it was an impossibility? She and Amos did not even share the same bed, and as far as she was concerned, they never would. No matter how badly she might want a baby, it was simply not meant to be.

Mom reached out and touched Miriam's arm with her hand. "I can see that I have upset you. You and Amos have only been married a little over three months. You still have plenty of time to conceive. You must remember to be patient. Children will come in God's time."

"I really must be getting home now," Miriam said. "Amos took Mary Ellen into town, and they will be arriving back home soon. I need to get supper going."

Mom nodded. "Come see us again soon, Daughter. Bring Mary Ellen next time. She can play with Rebekah."

Miriam didn't argue with her mother, though she was wondering just how much playing two little girls could do when one of them was in a wheelchair. "*Jah,* I will bring Mary Ellen by soon," she said. She started for the door, then came back and impulsively gave her mother a kiss on the cheek. "Please do not say anything to Amos about me not being pregnant yet. It might upset him."

"Of course not," Mom said. "I will not mention it to anyone, but I will be praying about it. My heart longs for many grandchildren, just as I am sure that your heart longs to be a mother."

thirty-one

The summer went by more quickly than Miriam had expected it to. There had been so much to do. Planting, weeding, and harvesting all the garden produce. Then came canning, making jellies and apple butter, besides all of the usual home and farm chores.

Mary Ellen had grown so much over the summer that Miriam had to make her several new school dresses. She hadn't realized how demanding the role of motherhood would be, but much to her surprise, she found herself enjoying it. It caused her heart to ache even more for a child of her own.

She often found herself thinking about William Graber and the love they had once shared. If they had married as planned, she would no doubt have one or two children already. She knew that she couldn't allow herself to dwell on that. The past was in the past, and now she had a new life to think about. Mary Ellen needed her, and she would be the only child Miriam would ever raise. Being around Mary Ellen had given her a reason to laugh and smile again.

Miriam even found that she was becoming more relaxed around Amos. He was a soft-spoken man with an easy, pleasant way about him. Though he wasn't what she would consider good-looking, he certainly wasn't ugly, either. Being near him did not make her heart pound wildly in her chest the way it had whenever she was with William, or even Nick, but at least she could feel respect for Amos Hilty, which was something William Graber had certainly not earned.

One evening, just a few days before school began again, Amos was reading the Bible. "We will be reading in Psalms," he said. "Chapter one hundred and twenty-seven, verses three through five say, 'Lo, children are an heritage of the Lord: and the fruit of the womb is his reward. As arrows are in the

142

hand of a mighty man; so are children of the youth. Happy is the man that has his quiver full of them.' "

Mary Ellen gave her father a puzzled look. "What is a quiver, Pappy?"

Amos stroked his beard thoughtfully, then answered, "A quiver is a case for carrying arrows."

"Do you have a quiver, Pappy?"

Amos smiled and reached out to place a large hand on the top of his daughter's head. "I have no case full of arrows, but I do have a home, and God's Word is saying that men are happy when they have a home full of children."

Mary Ellen frowned and stuck out her bottom lip. "You only have one child, Pappy. You must be very sad."

Miriam cringed and swallowed hard. Mary Ellen had hit a nerve. At least with her, she had. Miriam was not as happy as she knew she could be. One of the reasons for this was her deep desire for a baby.

Amos pulled Mary Ellen from her chair and into his lap. "I must admit, having more children would be nice, but I am very happy with just one. If God ever sees fit to bless our home with more little ones, I will not complain, but you are all I need if He chooses not to."

Mary Ellen smiled at her father. "I hope that God does send us a baby sometime. I want a little brother or sister to play with."

The tears that had formed behind Miriam's eyes threatened to spill over, and it took all of her willpower to keep from openly crying.

"If God wishes it to be so, then it will happen in His time," Amos told the child.

"Then I will pray and ask God to hurry up!" Mary Ellen said eagerly.

Amos looked as though he was about to say something more, but instead, he closed the Bible and lifted his hand to brush the tears that had escaped unknowingly from Miriam's eyes. When the back of his hand brushed against her cheek, Miriam quickly pulled away.

Amos withdrew his hand and stood up. "There are a few things outside that I must tend to," he said.

Miriam watched his retreating form with a great sadness in her heart. She felt a sense of relief that he had taken his hand away and left the room, yet it was mixed with a feeling of disappointment, too. She did not even bother to try and analyze her feelings, but she did know one thing for certain. Amos Hilty, her husband in name only, was as miserable as she was.

❧

Mary Ellen had been back in school for two weeks, and every day Miriam would either walk with the child or drive her to and from school in their buggy. She felt that the child was not yet old enough to walk alone, and she had changed her mind about letting her walk with some of the other children. Some of them who lived nearby had been among those who had teased and taunted Mary Ellen during school hours. Miriam could not take the chance that the teasing might continue on the walks to and from school. Besides, she found herself enjoying the extra time that it gave her to be with Mary Ellen when they either walked or rode together.

One afternoon, when Amos was out in the fields working, Miriam decided to leave a little early and stop and pay a call on Crystal before picking Mary Ellen up from school. She found her sister-in-law on the front porch, sweeping off the leaves that had fallen there. Crystal waved and set the broom aside. "It's so good to see you!" she called.

Miriam stepped down from her buggy and started toward the house. "*Jah,* it has been awhile, hasn't it?"

Crystal smiled and nodded. "I have been wondering about you. How are you doing now that school has started?"

Miriam plopped down on the top step of the porch and sighed deeply. "It is so hard to take Mary Ellen to school each day, then turn around and go back home to an empty house. Teaching the children has filled up my life for several years, and I must admit, I do miss it. It's hard to see Bishop Benner's daughter Linda taking my place as the new teacher."

Crystal sat down next to Miriam. "But you do have Mary

Ellen to train and teach at home. The role of motherhood can be very rewarding. You will see that even more when other children come along."

Miriam gave her a questioning look. "Other children?"

"*Jah.* When you have a few other little ones."

Miriam shook her head, but Crystal didn't seem to notice. She continued, "Ach, my, you will be so busy changing diapers and doing extra laundry, you won't even have time to think about schoolteaching."

Miriam's eyes narrowed. "There will be no babies for me," she said bitterly.

Crystal reached for her hand. "Miriam, it has only been five months since you and Amos were married. Give it some time, friend. It is God's time anyway, and it will happen when He is ready."

Miriam had confided in Crystal before the wedding, telling her why she was marrying Amos, and that there was no love between them. However, she had not spoken of the matter since then, and so Crystal obviously did not understand the full concept of things. Miriam was ashamed to tell even her best friend that she, a woman who was supposed to be a good Amish wife, was sleeping in her own bedroom, just next door to the room that her husband slept in. There had been no physical union between them, and therefore there would be no babies.

Miriam drew in a deep breath and decided that now was the time to confide in someone who might give her some understanding and sympathy. "I will never get pregnant," she whispered.

"Now, Miriam, good things come to those who wait," Crystal said with conviction.

A tear slid out from under Miriam's lashes and landed on the front of her dress. "Amos and I have not consummated our marriage."

Crystal's mouth fell open. "You mean—"

"*Jah.* We sleep in separate rooms. We are man and wife in name only." Miriam wiped the corners of her eyes with the backs of her hands. She hated tears. She saw it as a sign of weakness, yet she so often resorted to tears these days.

"Has Amos actually agreed to such an arrangement?" Crystal asked.

Miriam sniffed and nodded. "Of course he agreed. He knows that I don't love him, and he feels no love for me, either. Our marriage was one of convenience. He provides a home and food for me, and I cook, clean, and take care of his daughter."

Crystal placed a loving hand on Miriam's arm. "Miriam, he could have simply hired someone for those tasks. Surely Amos needs a wife and not just a housekeeper."

"Then he should have married someone else. Someone for whom he felt love." Another unbidden tear slid down Miriam's cheek. "I am afraid that I have ruined his life and mine as well."

"How can you say that? It is quite apparent that you care deeply about his daughter," Crystal said.

"*Jah*, I do," Miriam admitted. "She is a wonderful child, and I have come to love her a great deal."

"You see," Crystal said. "You just said that you have *come* to love Mary Ellen. It did not happen overnight. It happened gradually, and maybe you can learn to love Amos in the same way."

"But, I—"

Crystal placed her fingers softly against Miriam's lips. "Please, do not say anything more. Just think about what I have said. Pray and ask God to fill your heart with love towards the man you have chosen to marry. I feel certain that, with God's help, things can change between you and Amos."

thirty-two

When Miriam left Crystal's house, her heart was full of questions. She knew that Crystal cared about her and wanted her to be happy, and she even wondered if her friend could possibly be right. Could she actually learn to love Amos? Wasn't love a feeling that was simply there, or was it a matter of choosing to love, as Crystal had suggested.

Miriam tried to shake free of her thoughts and concentrate on the road ahead. The once cloudless sky had now darkened, and soon the heavens opened up and poured forth a drenching downpour.

Miriam turned on the battery-operated windshield wipers and tried to hold the horse steady. She had left Crystal's later than she'd planned, and now she was worried that she might be late picking Mary Ellen up from school.

As the rain came down harder, the air was suddenly filled with a thunderous roar. A bolt of lightning shot across the sky, just in front of the buggy. Miriam gripped the reins tightly and strained to see the road ahead. The small battery-operated lights on the front of the buggy did little to light the way.

Miriam found herself wishing she had not spent so much time pouring her heart out to Crystal. She might have been at the school by now, and the truth about her and Amos would not have been shared, either. She felt fairly certain that she could trust Crystal to keep the information to herself, but she still wondered if telling her had been such a good idea. She didn't want Crystal's pity, and she wasn't even sure that she wanted her advice.

Another clap of thunder came, interrupting Miriam's inner thoughts. This one sounded closer, and she shivered, both from the cold, as well as from her fear of the storm. Suddenly, there was a loud cracking sound, and the buggy lunged to the right. Miriam pulled back on the reins, calling to the horse, "Whoa now! Steady boy!"

The gelding whinnied loudly and reared its head. It jerked hard against the reins several times, causing the buggy to sway back and forth. It was dangerously close to the center line, and when Miriam saw the headlights of an oncoming car ahead, she gave a sharp tug on the reins. Another clap of thunder sounded, and without any warning, the horse reared up, and the buggy flipped onto its side, landing on the right side of the road.

The tongue on the buggy had broken when the buggy flipped, allowing the horse to break free, but Miriam was not as fortunate. She was pinned inside the mangled buggy, unable to open either door. She winced in pain as she pushed unsuccessfully against the door on the driver's side. Her side and shoulder hurt terribly, and there was a large gash on her head. She managed to rip a piece of her apron off, and she placed it against her aching head to stop the bleeding.

In spite of Miriam's predicament, her first concern was for Mary Ellen. She would be waiting for her at the schoolhouse, probably alone and frightened. *There must be some way to get out of here*, she thought. *Surely someone will see the buggy and stop to help. Oh, what about the horse? Is Amos's gelding all right?*

Miriam had no way of knowing that the horse was free and running down the road. She could see nothing out of the broken window of the buggy. The glass was too shattered, and the angle at which the buggy was lying hampered any possible view of the outside.

Miriam's head was throbbing. She felt helpless and alone. She was used to solving her own problems, and now she was trapped inside the buggy, unable to find an answer to her dilemma. A sense of panic began to overtake her, and she swallowed several times to keep from vomiting. "Oh, God!" she cried. "Please help me!" She closed her eyes tightly and began to think of Scripture verses she had committed to memory. "Second Timothy, one, verse seven," she recited. " 'For God hath not given us the spirit of fear; but of power, and of love, and of a sound mind.' Psalm twenty-three, verse four, 'Yea, though I walk through the valley of the shadow of death, I will fear no evil: for thou art with me; thy rod and thy staff they comfort me.' Mark four, verse forty, 'And he said unto them, Why are ye so fearful? How is it that ye have no faith?' "

Miriam took a deep breath and tried to relax. A sudden sense of peace came over her. She had been so far from God for such a long time, yet now she was keenly aware that she was not alone. The Lord was with her, and she had nothing to fear. She closed her eyes and drifted into a restful sleep.

"Miriam, can you hear me? Are you all right?"

Miriam's eyes opened with a start when she heard a man's voice calling out to her. She winced in pain as she tried to sit up straight. It was impossible, and then she remembered that the buggy was on its side. Had she been asleep? For how long? Was someone calling to her?

The voice came again. "Miriam, please answer me!"

She recognized the voice this time. It was Amos. Her husband had come to her aid.

"I am here," Miriam called. "I'm hurt, but I do not think it is too serious."

"I can't get the door of the buggy open," Amos called back. "I will have to go for help. Can you hang on for a little while longer?"

"*Jah,* I will be fine," Miriam said loudly. Then to herself, she whispered, "I am not alone—not any longer." She drifted off again.

❧

"I love you, Miriam. I love you, Miriam. . ." The words ran through her mind again and again as she tried to become fully awake and focus on her surroundings. Where was she? Who had whispered those words of love to her? Why were her eyes so heavy? Her head was pounding, too. Was she having another one of her sick headaches? She tried to sit up, but found that she was unable to. A terrible pain ripped through her left side.

"You had better lie still," a woman's voice said.

Miriam's eyes finally came fully open. "Where am I?"

The woman, who was dressed in a white uniform, placed a gentle hand on Miriam's arm and answered, "You're in the hospital. You were brought here when your buggy got turned over in the storm."

Miriam frowned as the memory of the whole ordeal came back to her. "It was so awful. The wind was blowing hard, and the lightning and thunder spooked my horse. I knew I would be late picking up my daughter, and—" Her daughter? Had she just referred to Mary Ellen as her daughter? Perhaps she was only just a stepchild, but she was the only child Miriam would ever have, and she had come to love her as a daughter.

"Mary Ellen. Is Mary Ellen all right?" Miriam asked, as she tried to sit up again.

The nurse placed a firm, but caring hand on Miriam again to keep her lying down. "Your husband and daughter are waiting in the visitor's lounge. They are fine and seem anxious to see you. Your family must love you very much."

The words "I love you" came back to Miriam again. Maybe Mary Ellen had said them. But why had she been called "Miriam" and not "Mama Mim"?

Miriam thought hard, trying to clear her cloudy mind. The last thing she remembered was being trapped inside the buggy. She could hear Amos calling to her and saying that he was going for help. Maybe she had fallen asleep and merely dreamed the words of love. Her heart was so full of questions.

"How did I get here?" Miriam asked the nurse.

"You were brought in an ambulance."

"When can I go home?"

"Probably in a day or so. You have a mild concussion, and the doctor wants you to be monitored for a few days."

"No wonder my head hurts so badly," Miriam said. "What other injuries do I have?"

"Many cuts and bruises, and some of your ribs are broken.

That is why your side hurts so badly," the nurse explained. "You are quite fortunate, though. Your injuries could have been much more serious in an accident of that sort."

Miriam nodded. "I would like to see my family now."

"Of course. I'll tell them that you are awake." The nurse moved away from the bed and quickly left the room.

Miriam shook her head slowly. "Did I just refer to Amos and Mary Ellen as my family?" Perhaps they were the only real family she had now. Since Mom lived with Andrew and Sarah, Miriam hardly ever saw her anymore. Papa was gone, too, and their home had never been the same without him. Lewis and Grace were married and living in the home where Miriam had grown up. They were even expecting their first child. Everything had changed so, and now Miriam spent all of her time and energy taking care of her stepdaughter and her husband. *A husband in name only*, she thought bitterly. A tear slipped between her lashes and rolled onto her cheek.

Miriam's thoughts were interrupted when the door to her room opened and Amos and Mary Ellen stepped inside.

"Mama Mim!" Mary Ellen cried. "Are you all right?"

"*Jah,* I am going to be fine," Miriam answered, as the child reached her bedside.

"You are crying, Mama Mim. Does your head hurt real bad?"

"A little," Miriam admitted. She could not explain to Mary Ellen the real reason for her tears.

"We were very worried about you. You gave us quite a scare," Amos told her.

Miriam studied his face. It did wear a look of genuine concern.

"How did you find me?" she asked.

"I was concerned when the storm came up," Amos said. "When you did not return home with Mary Ellen on schedule, I really began to worry. I hitched up the other buggy and started off for the schoolhouse. On the way, I came across your buggy lying on its side. I stopped to see if you were still inside, then I went to call for help."

"*Jah,* I do remember hearing your voice," Miriam told him. "I must have dozed off. I don't remember much after that, except waking up and finding out that I was in the hospital."

Mary Ellen's eyes were large and serious. "I waited at the school for a long time. When you did not come, I got scared."

Miriam reached for the child's hand. "I am so sorry that you were frightened, Mary Ellen."

Mary Ellen swallowed hard and a tear slid down her cheek. "When Pappy sent Uncle Lewis to get me, he said that you had been in an accident. I thought you were going to die and leave me just like my first mama did. I was very sad."

Miriam squeezed Mary Ellen's hand tightly. "I am going to be just fine. I will not leave you, Mary Ellen, I promise."

Mary Ellen smiled. "I love you, Mama Mim."

"I love you, too," Miriam responded.

thirty-three

Miriam spent three full days in the hospital, and during her stay she did a lot of thinking, praying, and soul-searching.

Amos came to visit her every day, sometimes twice a day. His daytime visits were after he had dropped Mary Ellen off at school, and in the evenings he always brought Mary Ellen along. Miriam knew that he must be getting behind on his work, because the trips to Lancaster took about an hour each time. She couldn't help but wonder why Amos was so faithful about his visits. Even her own family had not come to see her that often.

Miriam's injuries were healing nicely, and the pain in her ribs and head was beginning to improve. Her last night in the hospital was her worst, however. She had trouble falling asleep and had to ask for a sleeping pill. While waiting for it to take effect, Miriam lay in her hospital bed, staring at the ceiling and thinking about her life with Amos and Mary Ellen. Every muscle in her body felt tight.

At last, she drifted into a fitful sleep, only to fall prey to a terrible nightmare. It was a dream about Amos. He was driving the same buggy that she had been riding in the day of the accident. She watched in horror as the horse reared up, and the buggy rolled over on its side. She called out to Amos, but he made no reply. Her heart was gripped with fear that he might be dead. "Amos! Amos!" she called loudly.

"Wake up, Miriam. You were having a bad dream."

Miriam opened her eyes and saw the night nurse standing over her.

"I—I was only dreaming?"

"Yes," the nurse answered. "Sometimes the medication you took earlier can cause that. Here, take a drink of water and try to go back to sleep."

Miriam took the offered glass of water. "Thank you."

❧

Miriam awoke the following morning, knowing that it was the day that she would be going home from the hospital. She was anxious to go but felt confused about so many things, and she wondered just what her dream the night before had meant. Why had she had such a frightening dream about Amos?

She could feel the beginning of another headache coming on, and her hands were trembling. "What is wrong with me, Lord?" she cried. She turned over and buried her head in her pillow, giving in to the threatening tears.

❧

Miriam was dressed and waiting for Amos when he entered her hospital room later that morning. She was sitting on the edge of the bed, reading the Bible she had found in the drawer of her bed table. She looked up as Amos took a seat on the bed next to her, but she self-consciously averted his gaze, wishing she could simply disappear. She knew that she must look a sight. Her eyes were red and swollen from crying. They had been tears of confusion, of uncertainty, and of an unfilled need for love.

"Miriam," Amos said softly, "there is something we need to talk about."

Miriam forced herself to look into his eyes. "If it's about me not being able to do my chores—I am feeling well enough—"

Amos reached for her hand, and he smiled when she did not pull it away. "No, it is not about chores. I have been wondering if you have thought about what I said to you the other day?"

"What day was that?" Miriam asked.

"The day of the accident—right before I left to go get help."

Miriam gave him a puzzled look.

Amos looked deeply into her pale blue eyes. "I told you that I love you, Miriam, and I meant it, too."

Miriam swallowed hard. "I do remember hearing those words, but I thought I had just dreamed it. I was not even sure who had said the words to me."

"I have felt love for you for some time now," Amos continued, "but knowing how you feel about me, I was afraid to say anything before."

"Amos, I—"

He reached out and placed a large finger against her lips. "It is all right. You do not have to say anything. I know that you do not return my feelings of love, but I had to tell you the way that I feel. When I saw your buggy lying on its side, and I realized that you were injured, I was so afraid that I might lose you, and then I would never have the chance to tell you that I love you. When you did not respond, I thought that you might be angry with me for speaking the truth."

Miriam shook her head. "No, Amos, I was not angry. As I said before, I was not even certain that I had heard your words at all." She paused a moment, then continued, "I only wish that I—"

"It is all right," Amos interrupted again. "Maybe someday you might learn to love me as well. I am a patient man, and I'm so thankful to God for sparing your life. I need you, and so does Mary Ellen."

Miriam swallowed past the lump in her throat. "God is dealing with me, Amos," she said. "But I am not ready to make a confession of love yet."

"I understand," Amos answered.

"No, I do not believe that you really do," she said tearfully. "Real love means a yielding of the heart to another person. It means full commitment, loyalty, and trust. It is very difficult for me to trust a man, or even God. I have been hurt too many times. My heart has been filled with bitterness for a long time."

Amos nodded. "*Jah,* I know, but you have kept your promise and not let it show to Mary Ellen. I thank you for that."

Miriam sniffed loudly. "I really do love her, Amos."

"*Jah,* I can tell that," Amos responded. "I also know that you and your family have been through a lot over the last few years. You have suffered many hurts."

"*Jah,* perhaps more than our share," Miriam agreed. "But everyone in the family seems to have dealt with it well. Everyone except for me, that is."

"Why, Miriam? Why is there so much bitterness within your heart?" he asked.

Miriam wiped away her tears, then said, "I suppose my bitterness began when William Graber moved away and fell in love with someone else. I loved him very much, and he made me believe that all men are alike. They cannot be trusted. When he broke my heart, I vowed never to allow myself to feel love for any man. I could not even trust God anymore. He could have prevented all of my pain and heartaches!" A sob caught in her throat, and Amos quickly wrapped his arms around her and held her against his strong chest.

When the sobs had finally subsided, Amos lifted her chin and looked directly into her eyes again. "I understand your pain, Miriam. When Ruth died of cancer, I thought that my whole world had been shattered. I even felt betrayed by Ruth. She had left me all alone to raise our child. I blamed God for taking her, and I was very bitter and angry toward Him. I did not know if I could trust God anymore, but I was reminded that His Word says, 'I will never leave you, nor forsake you.' I hung onto that Scripture, and one day I woke up and realized that Mary Ellen needed me, and that I needed her. Life does go on, whether our hearts are bitter or filled with love. It is a choice we must make. We either choose to love, or we choose to harbor bitter, angry thoughts and feelings in our heart. Proverbs fifteen, verse seventeen says, 'Better is a dinner of herbs where love is, than a stalled ox and hatred therewith.' Hatred, anger, and bitterness are all negative feelings that can make us ill. That is why the Bible says, 'A merry heart—' "

"'Doeth good like a medicine,'" Miriam completed the verse. "Mom has quoted that to me many times. I have ignored God's desire for my heart. Lying here in this hospital bed for the past several days has given me ample time to think and to pray. I want to yield completely to God's will, but I am not sure that I can. I am so afraid of failing and never finding happiness, Amos."

Amos ran one long finger gently down Miriam's cheek, tracing a pattern where the tears had fallen. "I am afraid, too, Miriam. Afraid of being happy again, but I do love you, and I want to make you feel happy and loved as well. I want you to be my wife in every way. I want us to have children and to raise them to know God and to trust in His Son as their Savior. I want our family to be full of God's love."

Miriam nodded. "I want all that, too, Amos, but earlier this morning, I was reading in the Bible, and John chapter five, verse forty-two said, 'But I know you, that ye have not the love of God in you.' I am afraid that hit very close to home. I know that I do not truly have God's love inside of my heart. I really have never completely yielded to Him. Not even when I was baptized and taken into church membership. I did it because it was expected of me, not because I truly had faith in God or His Son Jesus."

"Then why not pray with me now?" Amos asked. "If you really want His will for your life, then you can yield to Him right here, Miriam. Jesus is waiting for you to ask Him to enter."

Miriam nodded. "*Jah*, I would like that. I have struggled and tried to do things on my own far too long. I need God's love and His power within my heart."

Amos took her hand. "Let us pray together and ask for God's forgiveness and the indwelling of His Spirit."

Miriam bowed her head and prayed aloud, "Dear God, our heavenly Father, please forgive me for the hate and bitterness that I have allowed to take over my heart. I thank you for sending Jesus to die for my sins. I accept His gift of forgiveness and love right now. Amen." She lifted her eyes to look at Amos.

He smiled a soft, loving smile that warmed the last frozen place in her heart. "*Wass Got tuht ist wohl getahn* (What God doeth is well done)," she whispered.

It was then that a new realization came to her. Amos was

not William Graber, or Nick McCormick either, but he was a kind, caring man. He had told her that he loved her, and now with God's help, her yielded heart could be a loving heart.

thirty-four

Miriam took a seat at the kitchen table and ate a bite of the scrambled eggs that were set before her. For the first time in a very long time, she actually enjoyed eating. In fact, her whole world had taken on a special glow. She felt like a freed prisoner must feel after years of confinement.

"Thank you for fixing breakfast," she said to Amos, who sat across the table from her. "You really should not have let me sleep so long. I am perfectly capable of cooking, you know."

Amos smiled and looked at her with love in his eyes. "I rather enjoyed cooking the eggs. I have not done much in the kitchen since we got married. Besides, I want you to get as much rest as possible for the next few days. The doctor's orders, you know."

Miriam smiled back at her husband and said, "These eggs are delicious. My compliments to the cook!"

"Can we have pancakes tomorrow, Pappy?" Mary Ellen asked. "Pancakes with maple syrup are my very favorite thing for breakfast!"

Amos laughed. "We shall see, Mary Ellen. We shall see."

When breakfast was over, Amos excused himself to go outside and finish the morning chores.

Miriam opened her Bible for her morning devotions. She had decided to begin having a personal time with God each day. She turned to First John, chapter four. " 'There is no fear in love; but perfect love casteth out fear: because fear hath torment. He that feareth is not made perfect in love.' "

How glad she was that she'd decided to quit fearing love. She could love and be loved in return. She had nothing to fear now because she knew that she had God's love and Amos's love. The storm that had caused her buggy accident had battered her body, but the storm that had been deep within her soul for so long had battered her heart. She was grateful that she had given all of her bitterness and angry feelings to God and had asked for His forgiveness.

Miriam turned the pages in her Bible and began reading from Philippians, chapter four. In the fourth verse it read, "Rejoice in the Lord always: and again I say, Rejoice." On down, the eighth verse read, "Finally, brethren, whatsoever things are true, whatsoever things are honest, whatsoever things are just, whatsoever things are pure, whatsoever things are lovely, whatsoever things are of good report; if there be any virtue, and if there be any praise, think on these things."

"All these many years I have not been obeying Your Word, Lord," she said aloud. "I have wasted so much time thinking about all of the bad things that have happened to me, that I could not even see all of the good things that You have done for me."

"Who are you talking to, Mama Mim?"

Miriam turned to see Mary Ellen standing in the kitchen doorway. She thought the child had gone outside to play. She reached her hand out to her.

Mary Ellen obliged, and Miriam pulled her into her lap, being careful of her still tender ribs. "I was talking to God," she answered.

"You were praying? But, your eyes were open."

Miriam laughed. It hurt her ribs some, but it felt so good to laugh that she didn't mind the pain. "I suppose they were open, but I was talking out loud to God and to myself. I was thinking how fortunate I am to have you and your pappy as my family. I just wanted God to know how I feel."

"I am so glad that it's Saturday and there is no school today," Mary Ellen said eagerly. "I get to spend the whole day with my mama and my pappy!"

"Should we do something fun together?" Miriam asked.

"Let's bake cookies, then we can go to the Country Store, and after that we can go out to the barn and play with Pappy's new piglets, and—"

"Whoa! Slow down some, Daughter!" Amos called, as he entered the room. "Mama Mim just got out of the hospital yesterday. She still needs to take it easy. If we do all those things in one day, we will wear her out."

Miriam looked up at Amos and smiled. "I am fine, really."

"You may feel fine, but remember what the doctor said," he reminded.

"I know, and I will get enough rest," Miriam promised. "But I'll rest after Mary Ellen and I bake some ginger cookies."

Mary Ellen's face lit up. "Ginger cookies! They are my favorite!"

Amos laughed. "I think all cookies are your favorite, girl." He took a seat next to Miriam. "May I help, too?"

"Pappy, do you know how to bake cookies now?" Mary Ellen asked.

"Sure he does," Miriam teased. "He knows how to lick the bowl, and he is an expert at eating the cookies!" She stuck out a finger and poked Amos playfully in the stomach.

He smiled and reached for her hand. "It sure is good to have you home, Miriam Hilty."

"It is really good to be home, too," she responded sincerely.

Miriam knew that her physical injuries were not the only injuries that were healing. So was her heart. She knew that God cared about her, and she was glad that she had finally opened up her heart to His love. Since love was a choice, and not just an emotion, she could choose to love Amos in the way that a wife should love her husband. She was thankful that she had chosen him and not Nick to marry. She was certain now that a mere physical attraction would not have been enough. Her thankful heart was so full of real love for Amos, for Mary Ellen, and most of all, for God.

❧

Miriam had been home from the hospital for several days and was feeling stronger and more content with her life than she had ever thought possible. Amos was very protective and would still not allow her to drive the buggy yet, so every day he drove Mary Ellen to school and picked her up again each afternoon. One morning, when he had just returned from the schoolhouse, he entered the kitchen and found Miriam making a second pot of coffee.

"I was wondering if you would have the time for a little talk?" she asked Amos as he began to remove his heavy, dark jacket.

He hung the coat on the wall peg and rubbed his hands briskly together. "That sounds good, if a big cup of hot coffee goes with it. It's pretty cold out there this morning."

Miriam smiled. "I will even throw in a few slices of gingerbread to go along with the coffee. How does that sound?"

"Mmm . . .sounds good to me." Amos smacked his lips in anticipation and pulled out a kitchen chair.

"I have been thinking," Miriam began. "That is, I was wondering if it would be all right if I move my things out of my room and into your room."

"Are you saying what I think you are?" Amos asked hopefully.

"*Jah.* I want to be your wife in every way, just as God intended that it should be, Amos," she answered.

Amos stood up and crossed the room to where she stood at the cupboard cutting the gingerbread. He turned her around to face him, and looking directly into her eyes, he asked, "Are you certain about this, Miriam? I do not want to pressure you or rush you in any way. I know that we are getting closer, but—"

Miriam placed a finger against his lips. "I want to be your wife, Amos. With God's help, I want to love you in every way that a wife should love her husband."

Amos wrapped his arms around her and held her close. Miriam could feel the steady beat of his heart against her chest. "I love you so much, Miriam Hilty," he whispered.

"I love you, too, Amos Hilty," she whispered back.

He lifted her face gently toward his, and softly, ever so softly, he placed a tender kiss against her lips.

She responded with a long sigh, and they kissed again. It was a kiss that told Amos just how full of love his wife's heart truly was.

thirty-five

If love was a choice, then Miriam had made the right choice, for she found that her love for Amos was growing with each passing day. His tender, gentle way had always been there, but before she had chosen not to notice. Now she thanked the Lord daily for opening her eyes to the truth.

Miriam found that she hardly missed teaching anymore. Her days were filled with household duties that she now did out of love. Amos always finished his outside chores as quickly as possible so that he could spend more time with Miriam. Often he would help her in the kitchen or with some of the heavier house cleaning. They took time out to read the Bible together and to pray, which Miriam knew was one of the main reasons they were drawing closer to one another and to God. They also spent time talking over a cup of tea or coffee and a plate of cookies or a slice of homemade bread. When the winter weather would allow, they would go for walks, hand-in-hand, and their evening hours were spent with Mary Ellen, playing games, putting puzzles together, reading, or working on some craft.

Miriam had one particular project that she was working on, and whenever she had a free moment, she could often be found cross-stitching on it, just as she was tonight.

"What are you making?" Amos asked.

"Oh, it is just a small surprise for Mom," Miriam responded with a smile.

❧

One Saturday afternoon in the middle of January, Miriam suggested that they hitch up the sleigh and go for a little ride.

"Where would you like to go?" Amos asked.

"I think it's time to pay my family a visit. Let's stop and see Lewis and Grace first. Then we can go over to Crystal and

Jonas's, and last, we will call on Mom at Andrew and Sarah's. I want to take Mom the little gift I've been working on."

Amos raised his eyebrows. "A little ride, I thought you said. It sounds to me like you're planning to cover the whole valley!" He smiled at Miriam and gave his daughter a playful wink.

Mary Ellen, who was coloring a picture at the kitchen table, jumped up immediately. *"Ich will mit dir!* (I want to go!)"

Amos bent down and picked the child up. "Of course you may go, Daughter. It will be a fun outing for all of us."

Miriam bundled Mary Ellen into her warmest coat, cap, and mittens, while Amos got the sleigh hitched, then she hurriedly gathered up three loaves of freshly baked banana bread. She planned to give one to each of the families they visited.

The sleigh ride was exhilarating, and the snow-covered landscape was breathtaking. It felt good to be out and enjoying God's majestic handiwork.

Mary Ellen, who was cuddled under a quilt next to her parents, called out, "Oh, look—there goes a mother deer and her baby. Isn't it cute?"

"Jah, Mary Ellen. All babies are cute," Miriam answered.

"I wish I had a baby of my own to play with," Mary Ellen said wistfully.

"Someday when you are grown up and get married, perhaps you will," her father answered.

"But that is a long time off," Mary Ellen complained.

"Maybe Uncle Lewis still has some of those baby bunnies left," Amos said.

"Really, Pappy? Could I really have a baby bunny for my very own?" Mary Ellen's face was expectant.

"If it is all right with Mim, it is all right with me."

Miriam smiled. Amos had been calling her Mim ever since she had declared her love for him and asked to be his wife in every way. She liked the nickname that Mary Ellen had begun when they were first married. *"Jah,* if Uncle Lewis still has some bunnies left, you may have one, but only on one condition."

"What is a condition?" asked Mary Ellen.

"Well, this one particular condition is that you promise to help take care of the bunny," Miriam told her.

"*Jah,* I will. I promise!"

૨ટ

Mary Ellen knelt in the hay, next to her father. She would be allowed to pick out the bunny of her choice. Uncle Lewis had taken them all out of their cage so that she could have a better look.

Miriam stood off to one side, talking with Lewis and Grace. She handed them a loaf of banana bread and leaned in close to whisper something to the young couple, but Amos and Mary Ellen were too busy laughing and playing with the black and white bunnies to hear her.

"I can see that everyone in your family is very happy these days," Lewis told his sister.

"*Jah,* very happy," Miriam repeated.

The rabbit that Mary Ellen chose was the smallest of the litter, but it looked healthy and bright-eyed, and it was certainly playful. On the ride to Crystal and Jonas's, Mary Ellen had quite a time keeping it inside the box that she'd been given. By the time they arrived, the bunny, which Mary Ellen had already named Dinky, was tucked safely inside the child's coat pocket.

Crystal and the twins were out in the yard building a snowman when the Hilty sleigh pulled in. The boys jumped up and down, always happy to see their cousin Mary Ellen.

"I have a surprise in my pocket!" Mary Ellen called to John and Jacob.

The boys ran excitedly to meet her at the sleigh, and the three of them started off for the barn.

"Jonas is in the barn, too. He's busy working on his old plow. He wants to be sure it's usable before the spring thaw," Crystal told Amos. "I'm sure that he could use a friendly face about now."

Amos laughed. "Maybe it is time to retire that old thing. Floyd Mast has some good buys on the new ones he sells."

"I know he probably should buy a new one," agreed Crystal, "but Jonas is rather partial to the old one. It belonged to his father."

The mention of Henry Stoltzfus caused a sharp pain in Miriam's heart. She still missed her father very much. She would always miss him, she supposed. Henry had been a devout Christian man, and for that she was very thankful. Some day they would be reunited in heaven. That was something to be thankful for, too.

"Well, then, I will go see Jonas and leave you two ladies to yourselves. I am sure that you both have plenty to talk about. Women usually do." He winked at Miriam and gave her a playful poke on the arm.

Miriam laughed and lunged for Amos, but he was too quick. His long legs took him quickly out of her reach, and soon he was out of sight, inside the barn.

"It is good to see you so happy, Miriam," Crystal said, as she steered her toward the house.

"*Jah,* I really am happy now—more than I ever thought possible. I brought you some banana bread, and I will tell you all about it over a cup of your great-tasting hot cider."

❧

The last stop of the day was at Sarah and Andrew's place. While Miriam was looking forward to seeing her brother and his family, she was most anxious to see Mom and give her the gift she had made.

It was beginning to snow again, and Amos hurried Mary Ellen out of the sleigh.

"Wait, Pappy. My bunny is still in the box. I want to take Dinky in to show Rebekah."

"I will get him," Amos told her. "You go on ahead with Mama Mim."

The warmth of the kitchen was welcoming, but the heat from the stove didn't warm Miriam nearly as much as the welcome that she and Mary Ellen received from her family.

"What brings you out on this snowy afternoon?" Andrew asked his sister.

"*Jah,* to what do we owe this pleasant surprise?" Anna asked her daughter.

"Oh, Amos and I just thought it would be nice to take Mary Ellen for a sleigh ride on a beautiful, snowy day." Miriam smiled at her mother and then winked at Mary Ellen.

"I've got a surprise!" Mary Ellen said excitedly. "Pappy is bringing it in."

"What is it?" asked Rebekah, who had just been wheeled into the room by her mother. "I love surprises!"

"Everyone loves surprises," Miriam said with a laugh. "I have one for Mom, too."

"So, who wants to be first?" Sarah asked, as she pushed her daughter up to the kitchen table.

"Mary Ellen can," Miriam said.

"But Pappy isn't here yet," the child protested.

Just then the door opened, and Amos stepped into the room. He had Dinky inside his coat pocket, and the small rabbit's head was peeking out over the top.

"A baby bunny!" Rebekah squealed. "May I hold it, please?"

Mary Ellen reached inside her father's pocket to retrieve the ball of fur. She walked across the room and placed the little rabbit into Rebekah's lap.

Dinky's nose twitched as Rebekah stroked him behind one floppy ear. "Where did you get him?" she asked.

"Uncle Lewis gave him to me," Mary Ellen answered. "He still has three more. Maybe you would like one, too."

Rebekah looked up at her mother and then at her father with pleading eyes.

Andrew smiled. "If it is all right with your mom, it is fine with me."

Sarah nodded. "I think it will be a good idea. Of course, you must help care for it."

"Oh, I will!" Rebekah cried.

"And you must share the bunny with your younger brother and sister," her father reminded.

"I will, Pap," the child responded happily.

"Come, take off your coats and sit awhile. You must all be

nearly frozen," Anna said. "I will put some hot water on the stove, and we can all have some hot chocolate."

"Have you got any of those great-tasting peanut butter cookies you make so well?" Amos asked, as he helped Miriam out of her coat.

"I think I might be able to find a few hiding out in the kitchen somewhere," Anna told him.

When everyone was seated, and the hot chocolate and cookies were passed around, Miriam spoke up. "It's my turn to tell you my surprise. First, I have something for all of you." She handed the banana bread to Sarah, then she reached for her coat, which was hanging on the back of her chair. She pulled something out and handed it to Mom. "This is for you. I made it to show how much I love you."

Anna took the gift from Miriam. A small sob caught in her throat. "Oh, Miriam, it is lovely."

"What is it? Let everyone see," Sarah said.

Anna held up the beautifully done cross-stitched wall hanging. It read: "A merry heart doeth good like a medicine."

Everyone in the room liked it, and Miriam smiled and said, "It's so true, Mom. You have been right all along, and I just could never see it. God does want each of His children to have a merry heart." She reached for Amos's hand. "My husband helped me see the truth."

"Oh? When was that?" Mom wanted to know.

"It was just shortly after my buggy accident," Miriam replied. "I have not really had the chance to tell you all about it, but I've been working on this cross-stitch for the past few months. I wanted it to be a surprise for Mom."

"And it is a very pleasant surprise, Daughter," Anna said tearfully. "It is certainly an answer to my prayers to know that you finally do understand the importance of a merry heart."

"I know that God has been calling to me for a long time," Miriam responded. "I only wish that I had listened to Him sooner."

Miriam looked at Amos then. "Would you like to tell them our other surprise?"

He beamed, but shook his head. "Let's let Mary Ellen tell them."

Miriam smiled. "That's a fine idea. Mary Ellen, tell everyone what our really big surprise is."

Mary Ellen giggled, then her small face grew very serious. In her most grown-up voice, she announced, "On the way here, after we left Aunt Crystal's, Mama Mim and Pappy told me that I am going to be a big sister!"

"Miriam, is she saying what I think she is saying?" Anna asked breathlessly.

Miriam nodded and smiled. "*Jah.* I am expecting a baby in about seven months."

"Oh, Miriam, that is wonderful news!" Sarah exclaimed.

"I am so happy for you, Daughter," Anna added. "First Lewis and Grace and now you. Oh, the rest of the family should be here to share in this joy."

"We've already stopped by to see Lewis and Grace, as well as Jonas and Crystal. They've all been told," Amos was quick to say.

"Congratulations!" Andrew said, patting Amos on the back, then hugging his sister.

Anna dabbed at the corners of her eyes with a hanky. "*Der Herr sie gedank!* (Thank the Lord!) I only wish that Henry could be here now. He would be so glad to see how happy our Miriam is."

"Some day we will be reunited with Papa, but until then, he will always be with us—right here." Miriam placed her hand against her heart, so full of love and joy. At last she truly had a merry heart!

A Letter To Our Readers

Dear Reader:

In order that we might better contribute to your reading enjoyment, we would appreciate your taking a few minutes to respond to the following questions. When completed, please return to the following:

Rebecca Germany, Managing Editor
Heartsong Presents
P.O. Box 719
Uhrichsville, Ohio 44683

1. Did you enjoy reading *A Merry Heart?*
   ❑ Very much. I would like to see more books
      by this author!
   ❑ Moderately
      I would have enjoyed it more if _____

   _____

2. Are you a member of **Heartsong Presents**? ❑Yes ❑No
   If no, where did you purchase this book? _____

   _____

3. What influenced your decision to purchase this
   book? (Check those that apply.)

   ❑ Cover   ❑ Back cover copy

   ❑ Title   ❑ Friends

   ❑ Publicity   ❑ Other_____

4. How would you rate, on a scale from 1 (poor) to 5
   (superior), the cover design? _____

5. On a scale from 1 (poor) to 10 (superior), please rate
   the following elements.

   ___Heroine   ___Plot

   ___Hero   ___Inspirational theme

   ___Setting   ___Secondary characters

6. What settings would you like to see covered in
   Heartsong Presents books?_____
   _____

   _____

7. What are some inspirational themes you would like
   to see treated in future books?_____
   _____

   _____

8. Would you be interested in reading other **Heartsong
   Presents** titles?   ❑ Yes   ❑ No

9. Please check your age range:
   ❑ Under 18   ❑ 18-24   ❑ 25-34
   ❑ 35-45   ❑ 46-55   ❑ Over 55

10. How many hours per week do you read? _____

Name _____
Occupation_____
Address_____
City_____ State_____ Zip _____

Mistletoe, Candlelight, and True Love Await

Discover the joy of Christmas love with these collections of inspirational love stories—one historical and one contemporary—from eight cherished Christian authors. Trade Paper. Only **$4.97** each.

____ *An Old-Fashioned Christmas*

Historical Collection

Sally Laity—*For the Love of a Child*
Loree Lough—*Miracle on Kismet Hill*
Tracie Peterson—*God Jul*
Colleen L. Reece—*Christmas Flower*

____ *Christmas Dreams*

Contemporary Collection

Rebecca Germany—*Evergreen*
Mary Hawkins—*Search for the Star*
Veda Boyd Jones—*The Christmas Wreath*
Melanie Panagiotopoulos—*Christmas Baby*

·········· Presents ··········

Great Inspirational Romance at a Great Price!

Heartsong Presents books are inspirational romances in contemporary and historical settings, designed to give you an enjoyable, spirit-lifting reading experience. You can choose wonderfully written titles from some of today's best authors like Veda Boyd Jones, Yvonne Lehman, Tracie Peterson, Nancy N. Rue, and many others.

When ordering quantities less than twelve, above titles are $2.95 each.
Not all titles may be available at time of order.